SF Publishing
www.sfpublishing.com

Wolf Pack

A Cold Night

Book 1

Written and Illustrated
By
Victoria Odoi-Atsem
www.victoriaodoiatsem.com

SF Publishing

 Published in the United States by SF publishing.
ISBN (paperback) 978-1-7367459-1-5
ISBN (hardback) 978-1-7367459-2-2
Library data.
Odoi-Atsem, Victoria
Wolf Pack. A Cold Night #1
Victoria Odoi-Atsem.-1ST ed. P.cm
Summary: “When 13-year-old Izzy gets lost in the woods, she suddenly finds herself plunged into a world of magic and mystery as she and her friends' fright to survive."

SF Publishing

For Bella

CONTENTS

CONTENTS

Chapter 1
"It will be an adventure"

Izzy stared down at the white beads on her bracelet with the letters B-F-F printed on each one. The beads hung next to a large, black stone that had a single, clear crystal embedded in the middle. She rolled the final “F” bead around in her fingers and squeezed it so hard that it left an impression on her skin. Forever is an eternity filled with hopes and dreams until the day you realize forever can end.

“Hey, Izzy, did you pack your toothbrush?” Izzy's mother asked.

Izzy's mother stood at the stove surrounded by a light haze of smoke that smelled of cinnamon and vanilla.

She was wearing baby Drew on her back; he was nestled tightly within a colorful woven kente cloth wrap. She was gently swaying side to side, rocking the baby. The wrap was a gift from her father. Izzy was used to seeing her mother wear it as a skirt. But her brother Drew had taken it as his own. *Much like everything else*, Izzy thought.

Izzy looked down at her phone.

"Yes, Mom," she said with a groan.

"Good! I always forget my toothbrush!" Mom said as she turned from the stove and placed two perfect pancakes onto Izzy's plate.

"Thanks. Do you always have to be this cheerful so early in the morning?" Izzy said while devouring her soft, sticky pancakes. The warm syrup dripped down her chin.

"I'm just so excited about this camping trip. We've been cooped up in this house all summer. It will be nice to get out and get some fresh air! It will be an adventure," Izzy's mom said while handing her a napkin. She watched as her mom turned back around to the stove. She thought about the adventurous summer she already had. Instead of spending the summer on the beach and hanging out with her friends, she helped her parents move into and renovate their new home. They moved into a house far away from all her old friends.

In her new neighborhood, there weren't any kids her age and she missed her old friends terribly. It had been the worst summer of her life. To make it worse, just before school was to start, her parents decided to take her across the country to Montana for a camping trip. Izzy really wanted to go someplace tropical, but she knew that going on this camping trip was a cheaper option for her parents. Even though she didn't like it, she thought she would suck it up and pretend to be happy. After all, it was only for a few days. She looked down at her phone again. She sent a text message to her best friend, Ana, last night explaining to her about the camping trip and how they might not be able to talk for a few days.

But her friend had not texted back yet. Ana had been taking longer than usual to text back since she moved out of the old neighborhood, but this was the longest. She sat staring at the phone, willing a message to come through. Bam! The front door slammed, waking Izzy from her daydream.

"The car's all packed up. All that's left is the cooler. Is all the food packed?" Izzy's dad asked while grabbing a bottle of water from the fridge.

"Yes, everything is in there. Would you like some pancakes?" Mother asked while pointing to the stove with her spatula.

"No, thanks, I already ate," Dad said. Mother sighed and turned back to washing dishes.

Dad kissed Mom on the cheek, ruffled Drew's hair, and turned to Izzy with a big, toothy smile. Izzy's dad was from Ghana and would often rise early and cook a traditional Ghanaian breakfast for himself of "koko" (corn porridge) and "koose" (plantain, and rice fritters). He always said American breakfast was like dessert. Izzy looked lovingly at her father, whom she nicknamed big bear, partly because of his size and partly because of his legendary bear hugs, which telling from his grin, he was about to give her now. Izzy's dad grabbed her around the waist, picked her up and gave her a big hug.

"Good morning, princess," he said.

"Oh, Dad, please put me down." Izzy laughed.

“I'm not a little kid anymore," Izzy protested while taking a deep whiff of his aftershave. She loved that smell. It reminded her of the changes of autumn and evergreen trees, ever-changing but everlasting.

"Hey, you will always be my little princess," he said with a big grin. "Come on, help me take this cooler out to the van."

Izzy and her dad carried the cooler out of the house and down the driveway. It was still dark outside even though it was morning, the crisp air bit at Izzy's neck as she shuffled through the fallen leaves. The back of the van was completely filled with luggage, and there was a large tent tied to the roof. Izzy and her dad picked up the cooler and placed it in the back of the van.

"All right, let's go. We have a plane to catch," Dad yelled as he slammed the back of the trunk closed.

"Quiet!" Mother hissed as she carried Drew out of the house and placed him into his car seat. Drew managed to sleep through packing, breakfast, and cleaning up, Izzy didn't think her dad's yell was capable of waking him. She laughed as her mom glared at her dad who had his hands up, slowly walking backward, mouthing "let's go" silently. She thought her mom looked so beautiful even when she was angry. She could tame any bear. Izzy climbed into her seat and put her seat belt on.

"Ok, family, let's start our adventure!" Dad said while pulling the car out of the driveway. "Two hours until we get to the airport!"

"Two hours?!" Izzy groaned from the back seat. Izzy looked out the window at her neighbors' houses as they drove out of their quiet cul-de-sac. She thought about how these houses were so different from the ones she used to live in. Her old neighborhood was filled with townhouses, lots of people, and lots of kids to play with. She left behind so many friends. Her mom insisted that the suburbs were a better place to raise a family, and they needed more space since the arrival of Drew .

Even though she liked that her current house was so much larger than her old townhouse, the memory of the endless hours playing with her friends filled her with sadness.

She never wanted to move, and she never wanted a brother; she had asked for a sister. Izzy frowned at the thoughts running through her head.

"Izzy, do you want to learn some trivia?" Mom said, interrupting her thoughts.

"Sure!" Izzy exclaimed. She loved learning new things and maybe it would help pass the time. Izzy's mom pulled a book from her bag and began to read.

"There are 762 lakes in the park and 2,865 miles of streams," she said while holding up the book for Izzy to see a photo of a mirrored lake flanked by grand mountains and pink clouds.

"That's where you'll find me all day, fishing! Izzy's dad exclaimed.

"You know the La people were fishermen?"

"Yes, we know!" Izzy and her mother said in unison.

"Jinx," Izzy said, quickly rendering her mother silent. Her mother pressed her lips together as if they were glued shut, mumbled something while pointing to her book. Izzy waited a moment, reveling in the power she held.

"Mae," she said finally.

Her mother took a deep breath.

"Thanks, that was brutal! Ok, more facts," Izzy's mother said, opening her book.
"Over 400 deaths have been recorded

to have happened in the park since they started keeping records 100 years ago. From grizzly bear attacks, falling into a crevasse, and freezing to death, just to name a few," her mother read before her voice trailed off and her face twisted into a grimace.

"Whoa, whoa how about we take a break from the facts, ok?" Dad said with a nervous laugh. "The park is perfectly safe if you use basic caution and respect nature."

"Ok so...are we there yet?" Izzy asked.

"No." Her mom laughed. "It's only been 30 minutes."

Izzy sighed and reclined her seat back. She looked out at the changing landscape. Roadways dotted with houses gave way to dense forest for as far as the eye could see.

Izzy's eyelids grew heavy. *Freezing to death, what a horrible way to die*, she thought.

Chapter 2
"Minor bad news"

Izzy awoke to a sharp pain in her scalp. She opened her eyes to see that her brother was pulling on her long braids. "Drew, that's mine," she said as she gently pried his tiny, baby-soft, fist off her hair.

"Hey, you woke up just in time, we're almost there! Here, give your brother this bottle," Izzy's mom said, passing her a bottle of milk. Izzy placed the bottle in her brother's mouth, and he began to drink. Looking out the window, she could see a large, green sign with a picture of an airplane, that read

"Airport 10 miles." Izzy let out a sigh of relief. Her legs were cramped, and she couldn't wait to get out and stretch them.

They pulled the van behind a long train of cars in the off-loading area. Izzy waited in the car with her brother while her parents loaded up a cart with all their camping gear. When they were finished loading the cart, Izzy's mom pushed the cart into the airport while Izzy followed behind her, pushing Drew in his stroller. The airport was virtually empty this early in the morning; the smell of floor cleaners still hung in the air.

"Wait here while I check us in. Your father is parking the car and will be back soon," Izzy's mother said while pointing to a group of metal chairs. Izzy wheeled her brother over to the chairs and looked down at them. They looked hard, cold, and uncomfortable.

After being in the car for hours, she didn't feel much like sitting. Instead, Izzy wheeled her brother around the glossy, white tiles of the airport. The floors were so shiny that Izzy could see her reflection in them. She thought they looked like the crystal-clear lakes she saw in her mother's guide book. Drew giggled every time Izzy sped the stroller up quickly.

"We're all checked in, and look here comes your father, " Izzy's mom said as she pointed in the direction of the doors. Izzy's dad stood by the front doors and looked around. Izzy shot her hands up and began to wave them around, only stopping when she caught his attention and he began to walk over to her.

"Minor bad news," Izzy's mom said. "I was unable to get us all seated together. The plane is full, and we're the last ones to check-in! We have to get to security quickly and board; they're going to close the gates soon."

Izzy gasped. "Will I have to sit next to a bunch of strangers?"

"Well, you and Dad can sit together by the window, and Drew and I will sit in the middle seats. You will only be next to one stranger," Mom said as she began to push Drew toward the security checkpoint. Izzy frowned and groaned loudly.

"Don't worry, I'll take the middle seat. You'll only have to sit next to me," Izzy's dad said with a soft smile.

"Thanks, Dad," Izzy said as she placed her hand in his, and together they ran to catch up with her mother. Izzy and her parents walked down the aisle of the crowded plane, looking for their seats.

"Here we are," her mom said pointing at two empty seats on the left side of the plane near the window.

"Excuse us please," her dad said to a young girl who was sitting at the end of their row. They made their way to their seats and sat with Izzy near the window and her dad in the middle. Her mother and brother sat in the row across from them.

"Ohayo," the young girl sitting in the end seat said in japanese while leaning forward to look at her. Izzy looked down at the girl's outstretched hand with chipped pink nail polish. As she shook her hand, the girl beamed and swayed her short black and pink hair.

"Hello, My name is Kimberly, but everyone calls me Kay. My mom and two brothers are a few rows up, and I got stuck back here by myself. I was worried I was going to be stuck sitting next to some old guy! No offense," Kay said, looking up at Izzy's dad.

"None taken. Well, this is Isadora, but everyone calls her Izzy," Izzy's dad said, pointing to her. She waved. "Hey, Dad, can you switch seats with me so we can talk?" Izzy asked, swiping her hand back and forth between herself and Kay.

"Actually, there are two other girls around your age sitting near me, if you want to move over here you all can sit together," Izzy's mom said from across the aisle.

"Sure," both Izzy and Kay said as they stood and made their way into the aisle. Izzy's dad squeezed her hand as she pushed past him and whispered in her ear, "Maybe you can make some new friends."

Izzy pressed her lips together in a forced smile. She didn't want to make new friends, she just didn't want to be bored on this long plane ride. Her dad's comments only reminded her that she still has not received a text back from her best friend Ana.

"Hello, my name is Kay, and this is Izzy. We only just met, just now," Kay said while sitting down next to a girl with a round, pretty face and short, curly hair.

"Hi, I'm Toya and this is my sister Aisha," the girl said.

"Foster sister!" Aisha interjected from the end of the row. Aisha was tall and slender; she has the kind of height that was obvious even while sitting. She has long, wavy hair that flowed down her back. A small diamond nose ring and a henna tattoo that snaked up her arm.

"Whatever." Toya sighed.

"Would anyone like some gum?" Kay said, and brought out a large pack of pink bubble gum from her pocket.

"No, thanks," everyone said in unison which resulted in a shy giggle from the girls.

"That's fine. More for me," Kay said.

"So, where are you guys headed?" Toya asked, breaking the impending silence.

"I'm going camping at National Glacier Park," Kay announced quickly before Izzy had a chance to speak.

"Oh my God! We are too!" Toya squealed. "Please tell me you're going too?" Toya said, looking intently at Izzy.

"Yeah," Izzy said slowly, afraid Toya would squeal again.

"Oh my God!" Toya squealed again, tapping Aisha on the shoulder. "Can you believe this? What are the odds that we would all be going to the same place?

It's fate! It's kismet that we would become friends!" Toya said, grabbing Izzy's and Kay's hands.

"Settle down, Ms. Cleo. I bet most of the families on the plane are going to the same place," Aisha said with a smirk. Izzy couldn't help but laugh as the wonder washed from Toya's face and was replaced with disappointment.

"Don't mind her, she's just being a Scorpio, she can't help it," Toya said with an air of authority.

"Oh, man, here we go again with this zodiac mess," Aisha said while putting on her headphones. Toya pulled out a book entitled *Zodiac signs 101*.

“When is your birthday, Kay?” Toya asked, flipping through the book.“April 10th,” Kay replied, peering at the book.

“You’re an Aries! I love Aries, they’re very determined and confident. You’re ruled by mars,” Toya said.

Well, that's accurate. A super confident Martian, Izzy thought.

“Ok, Izzy, when’s your birthday?”

“July 1st,” Izzy said with indifference.

“Oh, you’re a Cancer. You’re very compassionate and empathetic. You’re ruled by the moon,” Toya said.

"And what are you?" Izzy asked abruptly. But she regretted it as soon as the words left her mouth. Toya smiled.

"I'm glad you asked. I'm an Aquarius. We are very intelligent. We're not only book smart but very intuitive. We are free-spirited and open-minded. We are visionaries and spend our time thinking about ways to improve the world and help people," Toya said.

"And what's your ruling planet?" Aisha asked, lowering her headphones.

"Uranus," Toya answered, clenching her teeth.

"Ha! The smartest planet in the galaxy," Aisha teased.

Izzy pinched her lips tightly together as she tried hard not to laugh.

Izzy spent the rest of the flight watching movies and learning about the other girls' hobbies. Kay was very athletic and was into many sports including track and parkour. Aisha was very artistic, and Toya loved to read. When the flight reached its destination, the girls parted ways, saying goodbye and vowing to find each other again once they reached the park.

Chapter 3
"National Glacier Park"

“Did these bags get heavier?” Izzy said as she helped her father load their bags onto the airport’s luggage cart. Izzy helped her father push the cart outside to the taxi area while her mother pushed Drew in his stroller. “This is us,'' Izzy’s dad said as he pointed to a man holding a sign that read “Asante Family”.

“Hello,” Izzy's dad said as he shook the driver's hand. Izzy and her family loaded their luggage into the minivan and shuffled themselves into the vinyl seats.

The van looked clean, but Izzy thought it still smelled of dirty socks. Izzy held her breath as she cracked open the side window that only extended out one inch, letting in the tiniest amount of fresh air.

"Don't worry, we'll be breathing in the freshest air known to man soon enough," Izzy's dad reassured her. She laid her head on her father's broad shoulder, and the van pulled away from the airport. Soon, the industrious scenery of the airport's grey building flanked in glass gave way to tall trees and mountains. Izzy looked out the window as the van turned onto a gravel road. The tires rolling over the uneven roadway were a stark contrast to the smooth, paved road they just left. The van rocked side to side as it crunched over the stones. The sound rumbled deeply in her ears.

Up ahead, Izzy could see a large stone and wooden sign that read "National Glacier Park". There was an emblem in the shape of an arrowhead. On the arrowhead, there were pictures of snow-capped mountains, tall trees, and a bison.

As they drove into the park, she could see tall trees and a crystal-clear lake surrounded by mountains. Izzy thought the pictures in her mother's guidebook didn't do the scenery justice. The beauty of the forest and mountains took her breath away. Izzy stepped out of the van and took a deep breath of clean, fresh air. The crisp, cool air filled her lungs and gave her a sense of home. Izzy stood frozen, staring off into the distance, allowing the strangely familiar feeling to wash over her.

"Mom, have we been here before, maybe when I was a baby?" Izzy asked.

"Nope, this is the first time for all of us. Why?"

"Nothing," Izzy muttered, looking around one more time.

"Please help me load the stuff onto our golf cart so we can go find our campsite."

Izzy and her family drove down a dirt road towards the campsite marked number twenty-two. Izzy looked around at their campsite, which was sandwiched between two large trees. There was a metal fire ring with a few logs and a hand-pumped waterspout. Other than those two things, the campsite was bare.

Their campsite was surrounded by several other campers who were in various stages of set-up. Izzy looked around, trying to see if she could spot Kay, Toya, or Aisha.

They did say they were camping here, Izzy thought as she looked down the path.

"Excuse me!" a little boy yelled as he whizzed by her on his bike. Izzy jumped back, tripped over a log. She would've fallen if it weren't for her father, who managed to catch her before she fell.

"Hey, remember what I told you? You always need to be aware of your surroundings,"her father said, looking at her sternly.

"I know, Dad. I was just looking to see if the other girls were camped near us," Izzy said as she helped her dad lay out a tarp.

"Hey, don't worry. I'm sure they're around here somewhere. This place is really big, but you'll have fun exploring it," Izzy's dad said.

Izzy and her dad began to put up the tent while her mother unpacked their other camping gear.

Chapter 4
"Sometimes I forget things for myself"

Izzy's mom entered the tent to find her sitting on the ground blowing up their air mattress. She had already finished blowing up one mattress and was working on the second.

"Hey, Izzy," she yelled over the loud sound of the buzzing motor.

"Yes?" Izzy said, turning off the pump.

"I need you to go to the general store and get me a toothbrush. I forgot mine, and your dad went to check out the fishing lake," Izzy's mom said.

Izzy bust out laughing, falling over onto the air mattress.

"How is that even possible? You reminded me like ten times?" Izzy said while holding her side from the pain of laughter.

"Hush now," her mom said, swatting her butt with pretend anger.

"I have to remember everything for everyone, sometimes I forget things for myself," Izzy's mom said, helping her up.

"Now, this is where we are," she said, pointing to the site map. "All you have to do is walk down this path, when you get to the fork in the road, turn left and walk down past the RV campsites, the general store is on the left.

"Walk! Can't I take the golf cart?" Izzy balked.

"Ha," Izzy's mom said dryly, giving her a look that said she was not amused.

"Now go, hurry back," she said, handing Izzy a five-dollar bill. "I'm going to put Drew down for a nap."

Izzy grabbed her phone, exited the tent, and began to walk down the path, looking at the map. Izzy strolled down the path, crushing fallen leaves under her feet. She looked at the other campsites, searching for her friends, but didn't see anyone among the many families she passed. Izzy made her way past the RV campsites. At the end of the path loomed a large, wooden building that looked like it belonged in the wild west. Anchored on the roof was a simple sign that read "General Store" and below it on the porch were two rocking chairs that were occupied by two stuffed bears. Izzy walked widely around the chairs, imagining that at any moment the bears could spring back to life. As she pushed open the door, she heard the tinkling sound of a bell. She looked up to see a small, brass bell fastened to the door frame. Izzy walked forward, looking at all the many supplies available.

"May I help you?" a voice said behind her. Izzy turned around to see an old woman standing behind her. She had on a red plaid vest and wore her hair in a single long braid. Izzy stared behind the woman, trying to figure out where she had emerged from.

"Um, I was just looking for a toothbrush, do you have any?" Izzy asked, darting her eyes around the store.

"We have some free ones here if you're not looking for anything fancy," she said, pointing to a basket on her desk.

"Yes, I'll take one of those," Izzy said.

"You'd be surprised how many people forget their toothbrush!

Here, take one of these program flyers with you. It will tell you all about what's going on around the park. Tonight, we'll be having a bonfire with storytelling sponsored by the local Black foot tribe. It's very popular," the store clerk said, handing Izzy a piece of paper.

"Thanks. There's one more thing. Do you know a good place to get cellphone service?" Izzy asked.

"It's real spotty out here. Usually the higher you go the better it gets, but even then it's hit or miss. I suggest you just put away your phone for the weekend and enjoy nature."

Izzy thanked the clerk again and headed back down the path to her campsite.

Izzy arrived back at the campsite to see her father cooking on their grill and her mother sitting by the fire with her brother Drew.

“What's for dinner?" Izzy asked her dad.

"Hotdogs and corn on the cob should be ready in just a minute," Izzy's dad said.

Izzy sat in an empty chair near her mother and began to play peek-a-boo with her brother. She could smell the hotdogs cooking on the grill and it made her mouth water. The sound of the pops and cracking of the burning charcoal reminded Izzy of the bonfire the store clerk told her about.

"Mom, after dinner can we go to the bonfire they are having? The store clerk told me about it," Izzy asked.

Her mother nodded, looking at the event flyer Izzy handed her.

"That sounds like fun. By the way, did you get me a toothbrush?" Izzy's mom asked.

"Oh, yeah I forgot," Izzy said, reaching into her pocket for the toothbrush. "They had some free ones there." She handed her mother the five-dollar bill.

"Thanks. You can keep the money. Buy yourself some snacks or something," Izzy's mom said.

Chapter 5
"Always be aware of your surroundings"

After eating dinner, Izzy and her family loaded up into the golf cart and headed to the bonfire. Izzy looked around at the bonfire. There was a large fire in the middle of a field. It was encircled by several logs and benches for people to sit. Izzy could hear the snap and popping of burning wood. The smell of the fire was comforting and reminded Izzy of the smell of the fireplace in their new home. Izzy spotted an empty bench and quickly darted to it to claim it for her family.

Suddenly, she heard her name being called from behind her. She turned to see a flash of pink running up to her. It was Kay. Izzy smiled as she waited for her. Kay stopped just before reaching Izzy and did a series of flips before landing squarely in front of Izzy.

"I thought that was you," Kay said, wiping her hand on her pink leggings.

"Wow, that was impressive," Izzy said.

"Allstar remember?" she said while posing as if she was ready to receive a gold medal.

"Yeah, I've been looking for you guys all day," Izzy confessed.

“We must be camped in different sections. You want to walk around the bonfire and see if Toya and Aisha are here?” Kay asked.

"Sure, let me ask my parents," Izzy said, turning to her parents. With her parents' permission, Izzy and Kay began to walk around the bonfire. They found Toya and Aisha on the other side of the bonfire, sitting on a blanket.

“You’re really dedicated to this pink thing, aren’t you?” Aisha said as Kay walked up to where she was sitting.

“You know me, an Aries, I'm always reliable and consistent. Isn’t that right, Toya?” Kay said.

"Yes, and Aisha is reliably a Scorpio!" Toya said, gesturing for them to sit.

"I'm just kidding, have a sense of humor," Aisha said while moving over to make room for Izzy and Kay.

'I'm glad we ran into you here. We should hang out tomorrow."

"Our parents signed us up for this teen hike in the morning. Maybe your parents can sign you two up also," Toya said.

"I'll…" Izzy was suddenly interrupted by the loud sound of drums.

"It's starting!" Kay squealed.

Izzy turned to look at the raised platform to the left of the bonfire.

Two people were standing on the stage with a ranger. The ranger stomped up to the microphone, wearing thick, black boots. The microphone squealed loudly as he began to speak.

"Good evening, everyone. I hope you all had a wonderful day in the park. My name is Ranger Jeff. Tonight, we have campfire storytelling as told by Mark Ross, who was the headline storyteller at last year's 'Tell us Something' statewide storytelling festival. This year's festival will be held on February tenth in Missoula. We invite you all to come back and join us for this wonderful festival of the art of storytelling with great respect and appreciation. I introduce to you Mark Ross," Ranger Jeff said as he backed off stage. The crowd erupted in polite applause

Mark Ross walked up the side step of the stage and to the center and stood in front of the microphone directly under the spotlights. He was a short, older man with a thick, gray beard.

"He looks a little like Santa Claus," Izzy whispered.

"Yeah, if Santa went on a keto diet," Aisha said, chuckling to herself.

Izzy looked back at the stage. *Aisha is right, Mark Ross doesn't look jolly at all*, she thought. The spotlights cast creepy shadows onto his face and shirt as he stood in silence in the middle of the stage. After the applause died down, he began to speak.

"Tonight, I will tell you a ghost story, but it is not your ordinary ghost story.

This is a true story. It takes place in the Paris Gibson Square Museum of Art, formerly the Great Falls Central High School. Legend says that the school is haunted by a boy who drowned in the basement swimming pool. But what many don't know is how he drowned. His name was Sam Smith; he had an ordinary name, but he was not an ordinary boy. He was the son of the school principal. Because he was the principal's son, many students resented and envied Sam. You see, they thought he was favored by the other teachers and treated better. Even worse, they thought he was responsible for informing the teachers about their bad behaviors, constantly landing them in trouble. Because of this, Sam was teased and bullied relentlessly. One fateful morning, the students at Great Falls Central High

School decided to play a prank on Sam. They led him down to the basement pool, under the pretense that a few of his classmates were going to hang out by the pool and listen to music. Have a little party. But when Sam Smith went down to the basement, the kids pushed him inside and locked the door. They turned off the lights, plunging him into total darkness."

Suddenly, the stage went black, casting Mark in darkness. The crowd gasped. Izzy felt Kay squeeze her hand. Izzy squinted her eyes but all she could see was the faint outline of Mark's figure.

"Sam pounded on the door," Mark continued from the darkened stage.

Somewhere in the distance, Izzy heard the sound of pounding on a door. Izzy and her friends looked behind them, trying to locate where the sound was coming from.

"Bam... bam... bam! Sam banged on the door harder," Mark said again from the shadows of the stage.

The sound of banging grew even louder all around them.

"Bam... Bam...Bam! Sam banged on for hours, begging the other kids to let him out. But no one ever did. The next morning, his body was found at the bottom of the pool. Some say he tripped and fell in the darkness, banging his head on the side of the pool. Others say he was so exhausted from banging on the door all day that when he fell into the pool his arms were too weak to pull himself out.

Either way to this very day, if you go down to the basement of the old Great Falls Central High School, you can still hear the pounding of Sam Smith on the basement door," Mark said as the lights suddenly came back on and everyone cheered and clapped. Mark bowed and walked off the stage. Ranger Jeff walked back onto the stage.

"Wasn't he just amazing?" Ranger Jeff asked. "Let's give him another round of applause."

"Tonight's campfire storytelling is brought to you by the Blackfoot tribe. The National Glacier Park works closely with local Native American tribes who have extensive knowledge of this area to conserve and maintain a healthy balance within this park.

We hope that you take the time out of your vacation to learn about the Indigenous people that have called this area home for thousands of years. Please stop by the Blackfoot heritage center to learn more. Tonight, we have Kalani Reevis and his family here as representatives of the Blackfoot tribe. Kalani would like to say a few words before we end tonight."

"Hello, thank you so much for coming out tonight. My name is Kalani, I'm here with my wife Apani and my sons Jason and James," Kalani said.

"They are cute!" Aisha whispered, causing Izzy to giggle.

"My family and I, on behalf of the Blackfoot tribe, want to welcome you to this great park.

Our people have called these mountains and valleys home for thousands of years. It was our tradition to live in harmony with nature by following the great buffalo. We ask that while you are here you enjoy the beauty of the land without disturbing it. We have a motto here, *Leave no trace*. That means to dispose of waste properly. Leave what you find, minimize your impact on the land, and respect wildlife. We know it's hard to come all this way and not leave with a souvenir so we have a gift for you. We have river stones taken from the Blackfoot River. We have used natural polished river stone for centuries in jewelry making. Please stay where you are and my sons will come around to you. Thank you," Kalani said.

James and Jason walked around the bonfire with a basket, passing out stones. When they reached Izzy and her friends, Izzy looked into the basket of colorful stones. She slipped her hand into the basket and felt the smooth, cool stones pass between her fingers. She could see the fire flickering on the polished surface of the stones. Suddenly, a stone caught her eye. It was buried almost completely by the other colorful stones. Izzy pushed the other stones aside to reveal a stone that was completely round and white. The white stone had swirls of glittering pearl that sparkled in the light of the fire. I choose this one, " Izzy said, holding it up to the sky.

"Ah, a moonstone! Some believe that the moonstone has the power to reveal what is hidden," Jason said, smiling at Izzy.

"Ooo, did you see how he was looking at you? I think he likes you!"

Toya whispered in her ear teasingly. Izzy blushed.

"I'll see you all tomorrow," She said and hugged everyone.

“Don’t forget about the teen hike,” Toya yelled as they walked away.

Izzy showed her parents the moonstone and talked with them about joining the other girls on the hike as they headed back to their campsite. Izzy laid in bed, staring at the blue light from her phone. She tried to call Ana yet again but the phone just rang and rang until the voicemail picked up. “Just calling to say hi,” Izzy said into the phone as she tried to hide the cracking in her voice. Izzy drifted off to sleep, rolling the moonstone around in her hand as she buried her face into her wet pillow.

Chapter 6
"Someone please help me"

Izzy awoke to a crisp, cool morning with the sun's bright light shining directly into the tent. She pulled her blanket tightly around her as she looked around her bed for the moonstone. She found that it slipped out of her hand and rolled under her air mattress. Sitting on the edge of the bed, she unraveled the friendship bracelet that Ana made for her. Trying hard to remember what her friend had shown her, Izzy retied the bracelet string around the moonstone. She placed the black stone and the tiny beads that read BFF into her suitcase.

"Rise and shine, sleepyhead. Breakfast is ready!" Izzy's mom said, peering into the tent.

"Ok, I'm coming,'' Izzy said as she put on her jean jacket. Izzy exited the tent to see her family sitting around the campfire eating. Izzy sat next to her father, and he handed her a plate of eggs and bacon.

"So, did you think about what I said last night about the teen hike?" Izzy said between mouthfuls of food.

"Yes, I think it will be ok as long as you remember what I told you; always be aware of your surroundings and listen to the ranger," Izzy's dad said.

"Thanks so much!" Izzy said as she jumped up and threw her paper plate into the trash.

"One more thing," Izzy's dad said. Izzy turned around to find her dad standing behind her with a big grin. He hugged Izzy around the waist, picking her up in one of his legendary bear hugs, before gently setting her back down. Izzy ran into the tent to grab her backpack and water bottle. *Maybe we will have a picnic lunch*, Izzy thought. Izzy looked around the tent for something she could use as a picnic blanket. Izzy spotted the colorful piece of fabric that her mother was using as a baby wrap, folded neatly on her mother's side of the bed.

"I hope she doesn't mind me borrowing this," Izzy muttered as she stuffed the fabric into the bag. Izzy began to walk down the path to meet up with the other hikers. Suddenly, she had the urge to look back at her family. She turned around to see her mother and father sitting around the fire talking. Her mother had Drew on her lap, and he was watching the fire with great interest. Her mother laughed at something her father said. Izzy had the urge to run back to her family to hear the joke. Izzy shook her head. Stop being a baby. *You're just going on a hike; you'll be back by the end of the day*, Izzy told herself. She began to run down the path; she didn't want to be late. She rounded the corner and saw a group of teens standing in front of the general store. Izzy spotted her friends and walked over to join them.

"I'm so glad you're here. I didn't think you were going to make it," Toya said.

Just then the ranger walked out of the store and began to speak to the group.

"Good morning, everyone! I'm so glad you all got up early this morning to join us on this hike. I'm Ranger Jeff. Some of you might remember me from last night's bonfire. We will be hiking the Boulderpass trail. It is a beautiful path that will take you around Kintla Lake."

Even though Izzy couldn't see it, she could hear the rhythmic rippling waters that signaled that the lake was nearby.

"It is very important that everyone stays together and that no one falls behind. We will take frequent rest and water breaks.

Stay hydrated. When we reach the lake, we will break for lunch. Over here on the table, we have several different types of sandwiches, fruits, and chips. Please take one of each for your lunch. After you have selected your lunch and filled your water bottles, please meet me over here by the cedar tree so I can sign you in," Ranger Jeff said while pointing to a tall tree with red bark. Izzy and her friends selected their lunch, signed in, and followed the ranger as he began to walk down a trail. After a few minutes of walking, Ranger Jeff suddenly stopped and pointed to the ground.

"As you can see, here are some bear tracks," he said.

"Are there a lot of bears here?" Kay asked nervously.

“Yes, we have a large population of grizzly bears and black bears here. But as long as you follow a few safety rules, you will not have a problem with bears. Number one rule is don’t leave food out for the bears, clean up after yourselves so you won’t attract them to your campsite. If you do come into contact with a bear, make yourself really big and shout at it to go away, make a lot of noise,” he said as he held his arm up over his head, making himself appear taller. Ranger Jeff continued down the path, pointing out plants and trees as the small group followed him.

“You're still trying to get a signal?” Kay asked as she watched Izzy hold up her phone to the sky.

“Yes, the store clerk said I might get service on the hike since we’re going to higher ground," Izzy said, moving her phone around.

"So you just came because you wanted to use your phone?" Aisha asked, crossing her arms. "See, I told you, no one really wants to hang around you," Aisha said teasingly to Toya. Toya's eyes glazed over as she smiled, trying to hide her pain.

"Whatever," Toya said, pushing past Aisha, nearly knocking her over.

"Hey, it's not my fault I'm the only friend you have and I was forced to be here!" Aisha said laughing.

"Wow, Aisha that was mean!" Kay said as she chased after Toya.

"For your information, I came because

I do really like Toya. She is a nice person, unlike you," Izzy said, glaring at Aisha.

"Gzzzz, calm down, I was just kidding around," Aisha said with a smirk.

"Well, we better go find her! Ranger Jeff said we need to stay on the path," Izzy said as she began to head in the same direction as Toya and Kay. Aisha reluctantly followed behind her, kicking at loose rocks. Izzy and Aisha walked a short distance from the trail to find Toya and Kay sitting on a log. Toya's eyes were red from crying.

"Toya, I really like you. You and Kay are the reason I came on this hike. I have been missing my old friends and I was very happy to have the opportunity to make new friends.

What Aisha said was not true," Izzy said, hugging Toya.

Izzy glared at Aisha and motioned for her to come. Aisha, who was standing behind them, rolled her eyes and reluctantly came over to the group.

"I'm sorry, Toya, I was just joking," Aisha said unconvincingly and with a big, fake smile.

"We need to get back to the group before we get left behind; they're probably far ahead of us now," Izzy said. Suddenly, off in the distance, Izzy heard a faint cry for help. The voice sent a chill down her spine that made her body go completely still. Kay, Aisha, and Toya began to walk back to the trail but when they saw that she stopped, they also stopped.

“Hey, what's wrong?” Kay asked Izzy.

“Shhh,” Izzy hushed, turning toward the thick woods. “Did you hear that?” she asked.

Chapter 7
"We are going to freeze to death"

"No, I didn't hear anything," the other girls said amongst themselves. Izzy listened intently and stared deep into the woods.

"Help! Someone please help me!"

Izzy heard it again. This time it was clear, someone was hurt and called out in pain. Izzy took off running toward the sound.

"Izzy, wait!" Toya yelled behind her.

"Come on, I heard it again. Someone needs our help," Izzy yelled to her friends. She could not stop running, the voice was calling out to her but was getting faint. She knew if she didn't find them soon it would be too late. Izzy ran through the woods blindly toward the cry for help, tree branches wiped at her face and arms, her friends following behind her. Izzy stopped so suddenly that Kay nearly ran into her. She could no longer hear the cry for help, just a soft moan. She walked slowly toward the sound, trying not to riffle the leaves so that she could hear. Izzy stopped; she found the source of the cries for help. She stood shocked, frozen in disbelief as Kay, Toya, and Aisha crept up behind her.

"What is that?" Aisha whispered.

"It looks like a little wolf!" Toya said.

"Stay back!" the wolf yelled.

Toya, Aisha, and Kay jumped back.

"It just growled at us! We should just leave it."

"Do you still hear someone crying for help?" Kay asked Izzy.

Izzy turned around. "She didn't just growl, she said stay back. Didn't you hear her?" Izzy asked, looking intently at her friends.

"What? Are you kidding?" Aisha asked.

"No, she is the one that I heard calling for help!" Izzy said, pointing to the wolf.

"Come on, Izzy, you had us running through the woods and now we're probably lost all because of some prank?" Toya said, crossing her arms.

"I swear, I'm not pranking you!" Izzy said as she turned around to look at the wolf. Izzy stared at the wolf, looking deeply into its amber eyes.

"I know I heard you, didn't I?" Izzy whispered partly to herself and partly to the wolf. The wolf stared at Izzy for a moment.

"I can hear you too," it said.

"I must be going crazy," Izzy said.

"We both must be because I never heard a human speak before," the wolf replied.

"Why did you call for help?" Izzy asked.

The wolf looked down at his leg. "My leg is caught under this rock; it hurts so bad." Izzy moved closer to the wolf and bent down to look at its leg.

It was stuck in between two large rocks and looked broken.

"Can you help me?" the wolf asked.

"I will try," she said as she tried to push one of the rocks away, but it didn't budge. Izzy turned around to ask her friends for help to find them standing with their mouths open in shock.

"What is it?" Izzy asked, standing up and looking behind her.

"You, that's what," Aisha answered, taking a step back.

"What?"

“We just saw you talk to a wolf. You two were holding a conversation as if you could understand it and it could understand you,” Toya said.

“I know this is strange but somehow I can hear and speak to this wolf. Her leg is caught in between some rocks and I really need your help,” Izzy said.

The girls walked slowly over to Izzy, still in disbelief at what was happening.

“Just tell it not to bite me!” Aisha said, breaking the tense silence, making everyone giggle nervously.

“Ok, on three, we’ll push this rock over. One, two, three!” Izzy and her friend pushed as hard as they could. The rock moved, crashed down the side of the hill, through the trees.

"Thank you so much... Um, what is your name?" the wolf asked.

"My name is Izzy, and these are my friends Kay, Toya, and Aisha," Izzy said.

"Thank you so much, Izzy. Tell your friends I said thank you. I'm called Dakota," the wolf said.

Izzy turned to her friends. "This is Dakota. She wants me to thank you all for helping her."

"Izzy, I think I will need your help once more," Dakota said as she struggled to stand but fell back down again.

"I don't think I'll be able to walk, I can't get back to my family." Dakota winced as she began to lick her wounds.

"Don't worry, I can carry you.

Do you live far from here?" Izzy asked.

"No, not too far, just around that mountain," Dakota said, looking off in the distance.

"Dakota isn't able to walk. She asked if I could carry her home to her family, which isn't too far from here," Izzy told her friends.

"That's fine, but how are we going to get back to the campsite? We're lost out here and the sun is going down," Kay said.

"I don't know, maybe Dakota's family can help us get back," Izzy said. Izzy bent down and lifted Dakota into her arms, but immediately sat her back down on the ground.

"You are much heavier than you look!" Izzy said.

“I’m going to need help carrying her,” Izzy said to her friends.

“What are we going to do? It's not like we have a stroller or something,” Kay said. Kay’s comment made Izzy think about pushing her little brother Drew around and how she wished to hug him right then. Izzy's eyes lit up. “That's it! You're a genius!” she said. Izzy reached into her backpack and pulled out her mother's wrap.

“We can use this with some long branches to make a sling,” Izzy said as she held up the long, colorful fabric.

“Let's spread out. We need two long, thick branches,” Izzy said as she started to look around. After the girls found the branches, they laid out the fabric and together, they lifted Dakota into the middle of the cloth.

Next, they laid each branch next to the cloth and tied each corner onto the branch. Together, they lifted Dakota. Kay and Izzy were in the front, while Toya and Aisha were at the back. Slowly they walked deeper into the mountains with Izzy following Dakota's directions.

“Are we there yet?” Toya asked as she rubbed her shoulder.

“I think maybe a wolf's idea of ‘not far’ is not the same as ours,” Aisha muttered, stretching her neck.

“Come on, guys, it’s not that bad,” Kay said, seemingly unfazed by the steep trek up the mountain.

Everyone groaned at Kay.

“What?” she said with a grin.

"Just around this bend, and you should see the entrance to a cave," Dakota said after they have been walking for some time. As the girls drew closer to the cave, they began to hear growling.

"I think you better wait here," Dakota said. Following Izzy's direction, the girls gently laid Dakota on the ground. She slowly limped into the cave.

"So what do we do now?" Aisha asked.

"We wait," Izzy said, sitting on a boulder outside the cave.

"Well, I'm getting really cold. How long—" Aisha suddenly stopped speaking and slowly backed away as Dakota exited the cave followed by a much larger wolf. The wolf slowly circled Izzy with its head bent low, training its piercing yellow eyes on her.

Finally, after doing several circles around her, he spoke.

"Do you understand what I'm saying?" the wolf asked.

"Yes," Izzy said back with a growl, trying not to show fear. The wolf sat in front of Izzy and stared at her for some time.

"How can this be? Are you a wolf?" the wolf asked Izzy.

"I don't know how I'm able to speak with you, and certainly you can see I'm not a wolf," Izzy replied.

"Things are not always certain in these mountains. I have seen some very uncertain things in my time," the wolf snapped.

"I'm sorry, I didn't mean to offend you," Izzy said.

The wolf paused again, staring at her once more. "I'll forgive your disrespect this time since you are not a wolf and my daughter Dakota said you were brave in saving her. We wolves honor the brave," the wolf said as it began to walk back to its cave with Dakota. "You must go now. You have our thanks," the wolf said as they disappeared into the cave.

"Wait!" Izzy yelled, leaping off the boulder.

Chapter 8
"Keep your wits about you"

Izzy stood in front of the cave. She could smell a damp, musty odor of wet fur. Izzy could not see inside the dark cave, but she could hear the growls and movements of many wolves.

"We need your help," Izzy said into the dank darkness but there was no reply. The entrance of the cave was not tall, so Izzy had to get on her knees to crawl inside.

"What are you doing?" Toya said from behind her.

"I need to go talk with them; we need their help," Izzy said.

"Here's some light," Kay said, handing her a small pink flashlight that she unclipped from her backpack. Izzy began to crawl into the cave. The flashlight only provided a dimly lit area a few inches in front of her. Izzy slowly crawled deeper and deeper into the cave over the bones of many small animals. The bones cut sharply into her hands and knees, so she tried to brush the bones to the side as she crawled over them. Izzy was surprised at how deep the cave was because from the outside, it did not look so big. The air grew colder and more pungent as she crawled deeper. Suddenly, Izzy stopped. Although she couldn't see the wolves a few feet in front of her, she could feel that they were there. Izzy sat back on her heels and slowly raised her flashlight.

Izzy gasped as she saw that she was surrounded by a pack of at least ten wolves. Several wolves silently crept up behind her, completely blocking off any escape. The wolf that had talked to her outside slowly entered the circle.

"There is a fine line between bravery and stupidity," the wolf growled.

"I know you're no wolf, but are you a fool?" the wolf asked, snapping at Izzy.

"No, I'm not a fool, but we need your help. The sun has gone down, we are cold, lost, and need help finding our way back to our campsite," Izzy said.

"There is no human camp around here; we wolves make sure we steer clear of any humans. I'm sorry, I can't help you."

"Please, we are going to freeze to death if we stay out here!" Izzy said, crying into her hands.

"I thought I was talking to the leader of the pack, but I was wrong. Leaders don't show weakness. The moment you show weakness that gives your enemy their opportunity to attack," the wolf sneered at Izzy, as he signaled for the wolves to move in. The wolves slowly began to creep closer to Izzy, growling and baring their teeth. Izzy was frozen with fear when suddenly a voice spoke from the shadows.

"But we are not her enemy. She is the savior of my granddaughter, that makes us allies and friends," the voice from the shadows said. The wolves gave a wide berth of respect as another wolf slowly entered the circle. The wolf coat clearly showed signs of age and its dull eyes showed a depth of many years lived.

“Crying is not a sign of weakness, it is a sign of someone who has been strong for far too long,” the wolf said, placing a paw on Izzy's hand.

“Don’t mind Alpha. Some young leaders don’t know that humility is the essence of strength. I know someone who can help you,” the kind wolf said. “I’ll take you to see Minerva.”

“If you want to get mixed up with that old witch, that's your business. I won’t stand in your way,” Alpha said as he walked away, leading the other wolves deeper into the cave.

“Minerva is a witch I have only heard stories about. I wish I could come with you but my leg still hurts a bit. Thanks again. I hope you find your way home,” Dakota said as she limped behind her pack.

"You can call me Luna. We wolves don't associate with witches, they can be very tricky and are not to be trusted. You must keep your wits about you when you are dealing with a witch," Luna advised.

"Why do you think she'll help us if you say she is not to be trusted?" Izzy asked, scrunching up her face with worry.

"My mother once told me a tale about this witch helping her when she was a young wolf. The tale is that if you have something to offer the witch, you can convince her to help you," Luna said.

"I don't think I'll have anything to offer a witch," Izzy said.

"You never know what can be of use to a witch," she said as she began to walk out of the cave.

Izzy followed behind her, racking her brain for something useful she has that she could trade with a witch. Izzy emerged from the dark cave and her ears erupted with the sounds of the night. The quiet chirps of insects and squeaks of the nightlife sounded so loud to Izzy after being in the cave that managed to block out the sounds. Izzy waited while her eyes adjusted to the moonlight that seemed so bright. Kay, Toya, and Aisha huddled together, shivering in the cold night air, wrapped in the fabric they used to carry Dakota.

"What took you so long?" Aisha said angrily.

"I'm sorry, but the wolves can't help us get back to the campsite, but they know someone who can help," Izzy said.

"Are you kidding me? You keep leading us around like fools!" Aisha shrieked.

"Aisha, calm down. Let's hear her out," Toya said.

"Who is this someone that can help?" Kay asked.

"This is Luna, she's Dakota's grandmother. She knows of a witch that lives in these mountains who can help us," Izzy said.

"Did you say a witch?" Kay asked with a curious creak in her voice.

Aisha laughed. "This is great, talking wolves and now witches! What's next? Our fairy godmother is going to whisk us home? I think you've lost your mind!" Aisha yelled at Izzy.

"Hold on, we all believe that Izzy is talking with the wolves. At this point we better start believing in witches too," Toya said.

"All I saw was Izzy grunting and growling with a wolf-like a crazy person! I didn't hear a wolf speaking at all! Did you hear it, Toya? Did you, Kay? This is insane!"

“I might not have heard it, but I know what I saw," Kay said.

"Me too," said Toya.

"Fine, and what makes you think this witch will help us? You said the wolves would help?" Aisha asked.

“Luna is convinced this witch will help. I trust her and it's the only plan I have right now, so unless you have a better idea, I suggest we go talk with this witch," Izzy said, crossing her arms.

"I do have a better idea. I say we try to find our way back to the campsite," Aisha said.

"We don't even know where to go, we could be walking deeper into the forest; that plan is riskier!" Izzy said.

"Well, I disagree. We're bound to run into our camp," Aisha said.

"I think we should vote," Izzy said.

"Fine, all in favor of going to a witch's den to ask for help can stay with Izzy. All in favor of finding our way back to the trail follow me!" Aisha said. As she stomped away, Kay and Toya didn't move. Aisha turned around to see that no one followed her.

"You're going to regret this," she said as she spun around and continued to walk away.

"Wait!" Luna howled as she sprung forward, eyes wild. But it was too late. Aisha screamed as she fell off a ledge.

Chapter 9
"We're lost"

She tumbled head over heels into the darkness, rocks and branches cutting into her skin until she landed with a splash in the lake. Aisha screamed again as the icy water hit her already cold body. The water seeped into her clothes and hair. Izzy, Toya, Kay, and Luna carefully made their way down the cliff to find Aisha soaking wet and shivering on the muddy bank of the lake.

"Aisha! Are you ok?" Izzy said.

Aisha barely shook her head "no" through her shivering.

"Aisha, you're going to go into hypothermia if you stay here. Please come with us," Izzy said.

Aisha stared in silence at the lake rocking back and forth with the water from her hair streaming down her face.

"I don't think I can walk, I'm freezing," Aisha whispered slowly through her now blue lips. You could see the fog of her breath with each word she uttered.

"I'll just stay here and warm up," she said as she curled into a ball and hugged her knees tightly.

"You have to get up. When you start moving, it will keep you warm. We'll help you," Izzy said as she tossed her mother's wrap over Aisha's shoulders.

Aisha pulled the cloth around her shoulders and began to stroke her arm like it was a soft kitten.

"This is so pretty," she said as she stared hypnotized by the colors.

"This is not good," Toya said.

"Snap out of it!" Izzy shouted as she stroked Aisha's shoulders. "You have to get up!"

Izzy and Toya pulled Aisha to her feet, rubbing her shoulders, and they began to follow Luna into the mountains.

Guided by only the light of the moon and Kay's flashlight, the five of them made their way toward a natural bridge. The bridge looked like a giant archway carved into the side of the mountain. Izzy remembered that natural bridges were formed from glacier erosion. The mere thought of glaciers made Izzy shiver.

She didn't think she could get any colder.

"Please don't tell me that it is snow," Aisha's teeth chattered in Izzy's ear as she pointed to a patch of white snow up ahead. That was when Izzy realized that even though it didn't feel like they were climbing, they had just walked steadily in a spiral, slowly climbing a mountain. The higher they went the more patches of snow she saw, until finally they were standing in front of a large cave entrance dotted with snow. Izzy looked up at the sky as a single flake of snow gently fluttered down and landed on her cheek.

"Remember what I said? Keep your wits about you!" Luna said as she stood at the opening of the cave. The entrance was tall and wide enough for the girls to enter standing side by side. They linked hands, took a deep breath, and proceeded to follow Luna into the dimly lit cave.

The sounds of crunching and snapping echoed through the chamber as they trampled over tiny bones. Izzy thought it was odd that the bones littered all over the cave floor reminded her of the wolf's den. *Signs of a predator*, she thought as a shiver ran down her spine. Izzy blew into her cold hands and rubbed them over her nose that had gone numb. The walls of the cave have hundreds of small shelves carved into them. Izzy couldn't tell if the shelves were man-made or arrived at their shape naturally. Each shelf was covered in broken glass and mirrors. All around the stalactites and stalagmites grinned at them like the sharp teeth of a monster.

"Into the belly of the beast," Kay said as she squeezed Izzy's hand tighter.

Once in the middle of the cave, Izzy looked up at the ceiling that was over twenty feet high.

There was a hole in the ceiling that allowed the moon to shine down on them. The broken glass and mirror stretched up to the vaulted ceiling. The glass twinkled in the moonlight and made the cave light up in a prism of glittering, speckled light.

"Minerva, are you there? It's me Luna, Arcadia's daughter... Hello," Luna said into the darkness. A rushing of movement in a dark corner drew everyone's attention. Izzy turned and narrowed her eyes, trying to see who or what was there. As Izzy's eyes adjusted to the light, she began to make out the silhouette of a large form huddled in the corner. The form was the same brown as the cave wall so it was practically invisible. The form slowly turned its head around to look at them. Izzy gasped as the bright yellow eyes caught hers. The eyes had a hypnotic glow about them, and they stared unflinching right at her.

"That is not human," Kay whispered into the eerie silence.

"Oh, but I am," the figure said in a melodic voice that was just as hypnotic as its eyes.

Kay, Toya, and Aisha gasped because unlike the wolves, they heard the voice of this creature. The form slowly turned its body around to face them without moving its head and eyes from Izzy. What was standing before them in the shadows was what looked to be a giant owl. As the owl moved toward them out of the shadows, it began to change. It stood up taller, its wings extended down into arms, its beak turned into lips.

"Don't I look human to you?" the witch said as she slowly turned around for them, all while keeping her head very still.

Izzy studied the witch as she modeled for them. She has long brown hair laced with feathers and small, sharp facial features. She was wearing a long dress of brown feathers with bell sleeves that hid most of her hands. Poking out of the long, wide sleeves were dainty hands with long, sharp talons. The bottom part of her dress completely hid her feet and legs, and as she turned around, Izzy could see the dress had a long feathery train. Izzy thought she looked more like a bird than a human being and she surely didn't move like a human.

"That is the creepiest thing I've ever seen," Toya whispered.

"Shh," Izzy hissed, poking Toya with her elbow.

"I think you look great; you look like a human to me," Izzy said.

"Really?" the witch said, tilting her head to the side.

"Well...except for the eyes," Izzy said nervously. The witch stared at Izzy for a moment as she tilted her head back up.

"Yes, you're right," The witch said as she turned to look in the mirror.

"The eyes are the hardest part to change. They are the windows to the soul, you know. One can change who they are on the outside but who they are on the inside will remain," the witch said. "The truth is, I'm not a human at all. My name is Mora. You must have known my mother Minerva. She was the greatest witch I have ever known. She was teaching me transformation spells before she died. I'm able to transform into nearly any animal.

Humans have been the hardest; you see, I have not been able to get close enough to one to properly examine them," Mora said with a heavy sigh.

"I'm very sorry to hear about your mother. I would have liked to have met her," Izzy said.

"Thank you, that was a very long time ago. But you all must be very powerful witches yourselves; your human transformation is amazing. I must admit that I'm envious," Mora said.

"But we're not witches, we are actually humans," Izzy said.

Mora spun around from the mirror so quickly that her dress floated up behind her and a cloud of dirt and dust flew into their eyes.

She crossed the short distance between them with a flutter and a glide.

"Humans! All the way up here?" Mora said as she touched Izzy's face.

"I knew there was something different about you all, but you do know magic," Mora said, lifting the necklace on Izzy's neck.

"What? I don't know any magic," Izzy stammered, wiping the grit from her eyes.

"This is a very rare moonstone, and this lacing around the stone is an enchantment to enhance the powers of the stone and the person who wears it. Very powerful magic," Mora said, lifting the necklace with her claws.

Izzy looked at the necklace in complete shock. Maybe the necklace was what gave her the power to hear the wolves

Chapter 10
"I did what I promised"

Luna paced back and forth in front of Mora, swiping away bones around her paws.

"We came here to ask for your help," Luna said after studying Mora with caution. "I have heard tales that your mother used to help those in need."

"Yes, we're lost and need to find our way back to our camp. If we stay here, we'll freeze to death! My friend Aisha has fallen into the lake and is on the verge of hypothermia. We really need your help!" Izzy pleaded.

Mora glided over to Aisha, who was sitting on the cave floor, wrapped tight in the cloth. With her eyes closed, her head was propped against the hard cave wall at an odd angle; her long, wavy hair now looked stiff. Izzy could see the deep rise and fall of her chest and a whizzing sound could be heard with each breath.

"Yes, this one does not look good at all," she said as she placed a long, feathery sleeve over Aisha.

"But I never knew my mother to be charitable. I can help you if you help me."

"How can we possibly help you?" Izzy asked.

"You have to let me examine you and teach me how to act human.

I need to perfect my transformation spell," Mora said without hesitation.

"So if we help you, you promise to lead us back to the human campground?" Izzy asked, remembering that witches could be tricky.

"It's too far and dark to go now, you will never make it. I can help you survive this cold night and then after you have fulfilled your end of the bargain, I will lead you all back to the human camp. Do you agree?"

Izzy turned to her friends. "The choice is yours and we must make it together. What do you all want to do?" Izzy asked.

"I feel we have no other choice but to trust her," Toya said.

"I agree, what do we have to lose now?" Kay asked.

Aisha simply nodded without opening her eyes.

"Are you sure, Aisha?" Izzy pressed.

"I'm sure," Aisha whispered through her blue lips.

Izzy turned to Mora. "It's a deal."

"Good! There is one more thing I need from you."

"What is it?" Izzy asked with a nervous look on her face as Luna moved closer to her side.

"The moon is not yet at its highest point, my powers alone are not strong enough to do the spell; I will need to use the power you have trapped in that moonstone," Mora said, pointing to Izzy's necklace.

"But if I give this to you, I won't hear the wolves anymore," Izzy said.

"That amulet only enhanced what's on the inside already. All you need to do is find another way to tap into who you truly are. Deep within, your power will always be there," Mora said. Izzy looked back at her friends who were now huddled together trying to keep warm. She crouched in front of Luna and threw her arms around the wolf.

"Thank you so much for everything, and please tell Dakota I will miss her," Izzy said with a heavy sigh. Izzy slowly took the necklace off and handed it to Mora. Luna tried to speak to Izzy but all she heard was a howl.

"Now hurry! Everyone, gather around the altar," Mora said, pointing to a large stalagmite in the middle of the cave. Mora placed the moonstone necklace on the altar and began to chant. After a few moments of chanting, Mora placed her hands on the stalactite that was directly over the altar, and it immediately lit up with gold symbols. Mora continued chanting until a single drop of gold liquid fell from the stalactite onto the moonstone. Suddenly, Mora stopped chanting and turned to the girls.

"Now sleep."

Chapter 11
"Tell me what you hear?"

Izzy woke up to the warm sun on her face and the sound of birds chirping. She opened her eyes to see the sun shining through the tree canopy.

"Uhh, what happened?" Izzy heard Kay ask from behind her.

"I don't know. All that matters is that we're alive," Izzy said, still gazing at the sun.

"Ahhhhh." Izzy sprang to her feet when she heard Aisha scream.

"Aisha, what is it? Where are you?" Izzy said, frantically looking around for Aisha.

"I'm right here!" Aisha screamed from behind Izzy. Izzy spun around and came face to face with an angry wolf. Izzy froze in shock. She looked down at her feet to find two paws in their place. Izzy wiped her head around and stared at the tail that had sprung out of her backside. Izzy looked back at the three wolves that were seated in front of her.

"Toya?" Izzy hesitantly asked, looking at the first wolf.

"Um, hum," Toya said.

"Aisha?".

"Um, hmm!" Aisha growled.

"Kay?" Izzy asked the last wolf.

"Who else would it be?" Kay said while spinning around and doing a roll across the grass.

"I'm glad Kay is happy right now, but I'm not! What happened to us?" Aisha said.

"Well, it's kinda cool. My eyesight is so sharp, I can see everything!" Toya said.

"I don't know what happened. The last thing I remember is Mora saying she would help us," Izzy said as she looked back at Mora's cave.

"Mora!" Izzy yelled into the entrance.

"No need to shout, I'm here," Mora said. Izzy looked up to see Mora perched in a tree next to the cave. She was back in the form of an owl and has been silently watching them the whole time.

"We had a deal! You said you would help us!" Izzy said.

Mora spread her wings and glided down. By the time she reached the ground, she'd transformed back into a human, but this time she looked more human than she did before.

"I noticed I had the hands all wrong," Mora said, holding out her hands for them to see.

"We don't care about your stupid hands! What did you do to us?" Aisha shouted.

"I did what I promised. I promised I would help you survive the night, and here you are, having not frozen to death. I could have turned you into an owl—like myself. Our feathers provide great insulation against the cold. But I found giving flight to animals that are not used to it always ends in disaster.

Rabbits have great fur, very warm, but being prey has its own disadvantages," Mora said as she kicked the skull of some dead rodent at them. The skull rolled across the grass and landed at Izzy's feet.

"You know this is not what we were asking for!" Izzy said.

"I know no such thing! I have the power of transformation; did you think I would build you a campfire or something?" Mora chuckled.

"Yes, kinda," Kay said.

"Fire is human magic, I know nothing about it," Mora said as she turned to glide back to the cave.

"Well just transform us back and take us to the human campground like you promised!" Aisha said as she ran to block Mora's way.

"You promised to teach me how to act human first. Besides, I don't have the power to transform you back now," Mora said.

"Wait, what do you mean you can't transform us back?" Izzy said.

"In order to do a spell that big, I need to harness the power of the full moon or use a moonstone that has been charged by the moonlight. I used up all the energy in your moonstone last night," Mora said as she placed Izzy's necklace onto her neck.

"The next full moon is in two days. Now go enjoy being wolves, transformation can be fun. Meet me back here tonight and you can fulfill the promise you made to me. I need to go rest now."

"So what are we going to do for two days?" Kay asked.

"My parents are probably freaking out!" Toya said.

“Can we even trust Mora to turn us back?” Aisha shouted.

"Ok, everyone please calm down. We’re stuck in this situation now, all we can do is deal with it the best we can,” Izzy said.

“We are stuck in this situation because of you. Everything you lead us into turns into a disaster!” Aisha shouted.

“What? How is this my fault? If it weren’t for you being a bully, we would have never left the trail!”

“If it weren’t for you running through the woods like a crazy person, we would have never gotten lost,” Aisha said, leaping at Izzy and knocking her to the ground.

Izzy's body hit the earth with a dull thud and a sharp pain rippled down her arm.

“Whoa! That's enough!” Kay said, leaping between them.

“Move out of my way!” Aisha said, pushing hard against Kay, but she didn’t budge.

“Let's not fight each other, we’re friends, remember?” Kay said, squaring up in front of Aisha.

“Whatever.”

“It's just two days," Toya said.

"So what are we supposed to do? I don't know anything about being a wolf," Aisha said.

"But we know someone who does," Izzy replied.

Izzy and her friends walked back down the mountain to Dakota's den. Izzy marveled at how the ground felt under her four paws; the thick padding allowed her to step on rocks and twigs without pain. Her ears twitched at every sound, the buzzing of insects seemed so much louder now, and the world smelled so different to her. She could smell everything so distinctively, from the dirt under her paws to the tiny berries hidden in nearby bushes. Everything smelled so much that it was making her dizzy.

As they approached Dakota's home, they could see three wolves lying on the ground outside the cave.

"Izzy, is that really you?" Dakota said as she limped over to Izzy.

"Yes, how did you know?" Izzy asked.

"Well, you smell like you and you're still wearing your moonstone necklace," Dakota said.

"You are amazing. I can smell so many things but it's very overwhelming. Can you teach us how to control it and isolate different smells?" Izzy said.

"Yes, I can teach you all, everything you need to know about being a wolf!" Dakota said.

"It's nice to be able to hear you and talk to you now," Toya said to Dakota.

"Are you all going to be wolves forever now?" Dakota asked.

"No, the witch Mora will turn us back into humans in two days when the moon is full," Izzy said.

"Hmmm, two days is not enough time to learn how to be a wolf. We have to get started right away," Dakota said.

"Follow me."

Izzy and her friends followed Dakota down to the lake. Izzy looked into the crystal-clear lake and for the first time, she could see her new self. She had mostly grey fur, a thick, black line around her eyes, and splotches of white fur on the cheeks. Izzy thought she looked like she was wearing makeup.

She looked into the eyes of the face staring back at her and took some comfort in the familiarity of them. The moonstone necklace around her neck dipped into the water and sent a ripple across the lake. She remembered what Mora said about the necklace being made with powerful magic. Izzy wondered what Ana knew about magic.

Chapter 12
"Why does everyone look so sad?"

“First thing first! Wolves like to swim," Dakota said as she jumped into the water, splashing Izzy in the face. Izzy laughed as Kay, Toya, and Aisha jumped in after her. "Come on in, the water is nice!" Kay urged. Izzy looked at the glassy water and thought it looked cold. She slowly dipped her paw into the water. Izzy was shocked that she could not feel the water through her thick fur. Izzy backed up from the lake's edge and took a running start and jumped into the water.

"Cannonball!" she yelled.

Izzy and her friends splashed around in the cool water until Dakota got out and called them over to her. Dakota stood very still and stared down at the water.

"Shhh," she said as they came near.

Suddenly, she pounced and dunked her head into the water, pulling out a fish and tossing it onto the grassy bank.

"Lesson two, fish are great for lunch," she said.

"Ok, you have to teach us!" Izzy exclaimed.

"Ok, No problem. First you have to stand very still, so they can come close to the edge of the lake. When you see the fish, just dive in and grab it.

The trick is the fish is deeper in the water than what it looks like, so aim below the fish," Dakota said.

"You guys go first!" Toya said.

Izzy and Kay went to the edge of the lake and looked in. After a few moments, the fish began to swim close to them. Izzy and Kay pounced and dunked their heads into the water. Izzy resurfaced with a face full of water and no fish. However, Kay pulled out a large fish and tossed it to shore.

"Wow, that was impressive! On your first try!" Izzy said.

"Beginner's luck!" Kay said.

"Hey, do you two want to try?" Izzy said to Toya and Aisha, who were watching from the shore.

"No way," Aisha said.

"I'll try it," Toya said as she joined them by the edge of the lake. After a few moments, the fish returned and once more, the wolves dunked their heads into the water. This time both Kay and Toya resurfaced with fish in their mouths. Izzy was still unsuccessful.

"What seems to be the problem?" Dakota asked.

"I don't know, I just keep missing them," Izzy said.

"Close your eyes, listen to the fish with your ears," Dakota said.

"Listen to the fish? What do fish even sound like?" Izzy asked.

"Just close your eyes and listen, focus on what you do know," Dakota said.

Izzy closed her eyes and began to listen to the world around her.

"Tell me what you hear," Dakota said.

Izzy paused for a moment, taking a deep breath. "I hear the rustling of the leaves in the trees."

"That's good. Now try to ignore that sound, pushing it deeper into the background."

Izzy focused on muting the familiar sound of the trees.

"What do you hear now?" Dakota asked.

"I hear all your heartbeats and breathing," Izzy said.

"That's good, now again try to ignore that sound. Listen deeper."

Once more, Izzy pushed those familiar sounds into the background until she could barely hear them.

"Ok, I hear something unfamiliar, it kinda sounds like water sloshing around."

"That's them, that is the fish swimming. Now open your eyes, look at the fish with your eyes and your ears. Believe your ears more than your eyes. Remember the fish are not where they appear to be, so trust your ears."

Izzy stared at the fish once more, then she closed her eyes, dunked her head under the water, and grabbed a fish. Izzy resurfaced from the water with a fish in her mouth. The fish flopped around in her mouth and she could feel its sandpaper-rough scales rubbing against her tongue. She quickly tossed it on the pile with the other fish.

"I did it! I can't believe it!" Izzy said.

"That was impressive; your ears are very good, even for a wolf," Dakota admitted.

"Let's eat lunch, I'm starving," Toya said.

"You can have one of my fish, Aisha, I caught two," Kay offered.

"No, thanks. I'm not eating raw fish," Aisha said.

"Why not? It tastes just like sushi," Kay said between mouthfuls of fish.

"I don't like sushi," Aisha said.

"Shhh!" Izzy said, suddenly sitting up sharply. "I hear something," she said as she twisted her ears. I hear...the grumblings...of Aisha's stomach," Izzy said as she pounced on Aisha.

"Ha HA, very funny," Aisha said as she pushed Izzy off of her.

"Don't worry, Aisha, I have something for you. Follow me," Dakota said.

Izzy and her friends followed Dakota as she walked into the forest.

"Oh! Do you smell that?" Aisha said as she ran ahead of everyone to join Dakota, who was in the front.

"You have a really good nose!" Izzy said as she joined Aisha in front of a blueberry bush. The group went from bush to bush eating blueberries. Aisha stuck her nose in the air and started sniffing around.

"Hey, guys, come over here, look what I found," Aisha said.

"Wow, you found some raspberries! You're getting very good with that nose!" Izzy said as they began to eat the berries.

"Aww look what I found, a cute baby bear," Toya said.

Izzy turned around to see Toya snuggling with a cute brown bear with large, brown eyes. The little bear was snacking on berries too.

"Aww he is so cute," Kay said as she went to look at the bear. Suddenly, Dakota jumped in front of Kay, blocking her path.

"Lesson number three, stay away from bears!" Dakota yelled. But it was too late. Izzy smelled it before she heard it. A deep, pungent smell of musk and wet grass. Izzy heard the roar behind her. It was so loud the ground shook and Izzy could feel the tiny stones beneath her feet tremble. Izzy turned around to see a large bear standing on its hind legs. The bear dropped back down on all fours and let out another roar. Aisha leapt in front of the bear. She raised her back and let out a growl.

"Run!" she yelled.

Izzy, Toya, Kay, and Dakota took off running in the opposite direction. Izzy turned around to see Aisha running behind them. The group ran up into the mountains until they were sure the bear was not following them. Finally, the group collapsed on a ledge, exhausted.

"Did you see the look on that bear's face when Aisha just jumped out of nowhere?" Izzy asked, panting.

"Yeah, that bear was completely shocked and confused!" Kay laughed.

"You were fierce, girl!" Toya said.

"Hey, I'm Aisha, back down!" Kay laughed, leaping up with her back raised and growling. Kay's mimicking of Aisha caused everyone to fall down laughing.

"Dakota, how is your leg?" Izzy asked.

"It's fine, the swim in the lake actually helped it feel a little better."

"Who's up for going back and getting more berries?" Aisha asked with a grin.

Chapter 13
"I don't know much about bravery"

Izzy's ears suddenly perked up; she heard the familiar sound of footsteps. Out of the corner of her eye, she saw Aisha stick her nose into the air. Aisha has caught onto their scent, Izzy thought. Izzy twisted her ears to hear better and closed her eyes, trying to isolate the sound.

"Izzy! Toya! Kay! Aisha!"

Izzy's eyes snapped open as she looked over the cliff. "Someone is down there," she said. "Someone's calling our names!"

"There! Near that fallen tree!" Toya said. Everyone stared over the edge of the cliff and finally figures began to emerge from the woods. There was a group of people walking through the trees led by Ranger Jeff.

"Izzy! Toya! Kay! Aisha!" they yelled as they searched the area.

"That's my dad!" Izzy howled as she spotted her dad at the back of the search party. Izzy's howls startled the search party, and Ranger Jeff stopped and took his gun out of his holster as he looked around for them. Izzy let out a howl again, drawing the attention of the search party. Finally, they looked up and saw the pack of wolves looking over the cliff's edge. Toya and Kay let out a howl when they spotted their parents. Izzy caught the eye of her father.

"Dad!" she howled softly once more. But her father turned away as the ranger motioned for them to move on. Izzy and her friends watched in silence as their families walked away, continuing to call out their names.

"Come on, everyone, we need to get back to Mora," Izzy said as she watched her father disappear into the thick trees. Izzy and her friends made their way up the mountain toward Mora's cave. The sun was beginning to set and the sky lit up in beautiful pinks and purples. However, the group took little notice of the spectacle as they solemnly walked into Mora's cave.

"Why does everyone look so sad?" Mora asked.

"We're just missing our families. Are you sure you can turn us back tomorrow?" Izzy asked as she rested her head on her paws.

"Don't worry, when the moon is full, I'll have enough power to turn you all back into your true forms. I can even recharge your moonstone for you," Mora said.

Izzy wasn't sure if she could trust Mora, but she didn't feel like she had any other options. "Now it's your turn to live up to your side of the deal; teach me how to look and act human," Mora said.

Izzy and her friends sat in front of Mora as she slowly turned around in front of them. Dakota laid her head on her paws as they watched.

"First of all, that head thing you do is very creepy and not human," Aisha spoke up first.

"What do you mean?" Mora asked, stopping mid-twirl.

"Well, you always keep your head still when you're turning your body around. Humans' necks are not that flexible. They turn their heads with their bodies," Toya said.

Mora began to turn around again, and this time she moved her head with her body.

"That was very unnerving! Humans are so brave they don't need to watch their backs at all?" Mora asked.

"I guess that's a privilege of being at the top of the food chain," Kay said.

"Also, your facial features are all wrong.

You'll need fuller lips and a more rounded nose," Toya explained.

"And your dress... although it is very pretty, humans usually make clothing out of fabric, like this," Izzy said as she pulled the crumpled African kente cloth from the corner of the cave. The group spent the next two hours teaching Mora everything they could think of about being human and how to best blend in.

"Okay! That's enough. I'm tired of this, and I'm starving," Mora said as she turned back into an owl.

"I have to get going," Dakota said.

"Can we come with you?" Izzy asked Dakota.

"Oh, I don't think so. You're not part of the pack. I know Alpha won't allow you to sleep with us tonight. I'm sorry," she said.

"So where are we supposed to go?" Aisha asked.

"Don't fuss! You are free to stay the night here," Mora said.

"Thank you so much," Izzy said.

"It's no bother. I barely use my cave at night, I won't be back until morning anyway," Mora said.

"What do you do out there all night besides hunt?" Izzy asked.

"I watch." Mora stretched out her massive wings. "You'd be surprised what you learn by watching silently from the shadows" she said as she took off into the sky.

"I had a great day today; you all are the best friends I ever had. I'll come back in the morning and I'll put in a good word with Alpha," Dakota said as she rubbed her head against each of them. "This is how we wolves say goodbye."

"Good night," Izzy said as Dakota walked out of the cave.

Izzy and her friends picked a cozy spot in the cave and laid down, snuggled close to each other.

"I can't wait to see my mom tomorrow," Kay said softly through a yawn.

Izzy closed her eyes as she thought about her parents and her little brother Drew. She smiled as she remembered how he would giggle and pull her hair.

***

Izzy awoke to a drop of water hitting her face. The cold droplet slid slowly down her cheek. She opened her eyes and looked up at the hole in the ceiling of Mora's cave. Another water droplet hit her right in the eye, causing her to quickly close her eyes and shake her head. With her eyes closed, she could better hear the familiar sound of the pitter-patter of raindrops. Slowly rising from her position, she crept carefully to the entrance of the cave. She sat at the mouth of the cave and watched the rainfall. She stuck her nose in the air. She always loved the smell of the rain, but now the smell was even more intense. It reminded her of when her mother would do laundry and fill the house with the smell of clean clothes.

Mother Nature is washing the mountains, she thought.

"Beautiful, isn't it?" Mora said from the trees just outside the cave. Izzy looked up at Mora with a little jump, she hadn't noticed her before.

"You're very good at watching from the shadows. When you're in human form, you should try not to do that. It's considered rude," Izzy said.

"I wouldn't trade this spot for the world."

Suddenly, Izzy heard Dakota coming up the mountain. She had learned the sound of a wolf walking, and since Dakota's foot was injured, she resisted using that leg, which gave her a very unique walking sound. Izzy called out to Dakota with a long howl.

"Is that you, Dakota?" Izzy called out.

Dakota emerged from the brush with a big smile on her face.

"How did you know it was me?" She asked.

"I could hear you."

"Wow, you're really impressive. Where are the rest of the girls? I have some great news for you all."

"They're inside sleeping; let's go wake them up."

Izzy and Dakota ran back into the cave shouting, "Wake up, wake up!"

"Okay, okay, not so loud!" Toya said.

"Wake up, wake up!" Izzy and Dakota continued to bark.

"We get it already! We're up," Kay said as she stretched.

"Are you seriously doing yoga right now?" Aisha asked Kay.

"Downward facing dog!" Kay said as she stuck her tail in Aisha's face.

"Ahhhh, really?" Aisha said as she jumped up and pounced on Kay with a laugh. But Kay was able to wiggle away and took off running around the cave.

"Come on, you can't catch me,'' she said as she led Aisha around in circles around the cave. But Kay was too fast and nimble for Aisha to catch. The sight made Toya, Dakota, and Izzy laugh. Finally, Aisha gave up and collapsed on the floor.

"You're really lucky right now," Aisha said, panting. Which only made the group laugh more.

“I have some great news for you all. I told Alpha about how you were so brave with that bear, and he’s invited you all to come with the pack on our morning hunt!” Dakota exclaimed. “It is a great honor. Alpha has never accepted any outsiders to join the hunt with us before.”

“I would love to join your pack,” Aisha said. “Yeah, it sounds like fun,” Kay said.

“Okay, let's go. They’re waiting for us at the bottom of the mountain.”

“Just be sure to meet me back here before dusk. We have a long hike back to the human camp, and once we get there, I will need time to do the transformation spell,” Mora said from the shadows, causing everyone to jump.

“Don’t worry, I will make sure they are back in time,” Dakota said.

Chapter 14
"The sun has already begun to set"

Izzy and her friends quickly made their way down the mountain to meet up with Alpha and his pack.

“Which one of you is called Aisha?”

Aisha stepped forward.

“I am,” she said with confidence.

“We have heard tales of your bravery and impeccable sense of smell. Is all this true?” Alpha asked.

“Well, I don’t know much about bravery,

I'm just not used to backing down from a fight. I have always had a sensitive nose so I think the witch Mora's spell just enhanced that," Aisha said.

"We are always looking for wolves like you to join our pack; bravery is something every wolf must have. This morning it rained so tracking a prey's scent will be difficult. Are you up for a challenge?"

"Always!" Aisha replied boldly.

"Good, your friends can tag along too if they want."

Aisha turned and walked back to her friends.

"Alpha has invited us to hunt with his pack, do you all still want to go?"

"Yes!" everyone said in chorus.

"Remember that Alpha is our leader, we must follow his lead at all times. Stay behind him but not too far," Dakota said.

The group followed the other wolves as they began to walk into the dense forest. Aisha ran ahead to be closer to Alpha.

"Look here," Alpha said, stopping suddenly.

"Deer tracks," Dakota said.

"The advantage of hunting after the rain is you can find good tracks," Alpha said as he bent his head to sniff the ground. Aisha copied him.

"I smell blood," Aisha said.

“Yes, it’s hurt,” Alpha replied.

“So, this is the perfect prey to go after, right?”

“Not so fast. You smell that?” Alpha said, leaning down to sniff another set of tracks.

“Yes, but I don’t know what that scent is."

“Coyote.” Alpha narrowed his eyes and looked off into the distance.

The rest of the pack tensed and went on high alert, following the lead of Alpha. They fanned out, forming a circle, watching each other’s backs. Aisha looked off into the woods, trying to spot anything moving.

“What's going on? Why has everyone stopped?” Izzy asked.

"Coyote," Aisha said, narrowing her eyes.

"Let's move on, we don't want to cause trouble for our cousins, the coyote. Causing trouble for them will only lead to more trouble for us," Alpha said as he changed directions. Alpha walked a few more paces and stopped again.

"Rabbits," Alpha said, sniffing the tracks.

"Isn't a rabbit too small to feed the whole pack? I thought we'd be able to hunt something bigger," Aisha asked.

"We wolves don't hunt for sport, like humans. If we can pick up its scent it will lead us back to its burrows. Then there will be plenty of meat for us all," Alpha said.

Aisha nodded and began to sniff the ground, following Alpha. With their noses to the ground, they led the pack through the wet forest. Finally, they stopped at a dense brush.

"The trail ends here," Alpha said.

"I can smell them so strongly now, there have to be at least a dozen rabbits here," Aisha said.

"There is a group of rabbits grazing in the bushes over there. I need to split the pack into three groups. I will have one group go into the bush and scare the rabbits out while another group blocks them from going into their burrows. The third group will be our fastest runners, who will chase them down. Rabbits are fast, but if you keep on them, they will tire before you do.

We will form a U-shape around them, blocking their path and forcing them to go where we want," Alpha said.

The pack began to break into three groups.

"It's best for you four to hang back here and block the burrows. Spread out if you see any rabbits going for their hole chase them back, but stay close to the burrows, don't give chase. Dakota will show you how it's done," Alpha said.

"I'm pretty fast and agile, I can be a runner," Kay said, stepping forward.

"Great, we can always use more runners. Follow me."

Alpha, Kay, and four other wolves took up position in front of the brush.

"We will each guard one section of the burrows, just run back and forth in front of your section to block the rabbits from getting back in. I'll take the left side, Izzy takes the right, Toya and Aisha stay in the middle sections," Dakota whispered.

Dakota, Izzy, Toya, and Aisha watched as the rest of the pack crept slowly into the brush. Suddenly, three rabbits shot out of the brush and ran straight at Izzy. She jumped up and began to run parallel to the burrows, blocking the rabbits from going in. Immediately, the rabbits changed direction and headed back toward the brush, but the first group was blocking their path. The rabbits were now surrounded on three sides. They turned once more and headed in the only direction they could, straight into a clearing.

Alpha and the other runners took off after them. Izzy and her group watched as the runners chased after the rabbits until they disappeared from eyesight.

"Okay, now we track them. We need to find Alpha and the other runners just in case they need our help," Dakota said.

"I've picked up Alpha's scent, follow me," Aisha said as she took off running. Dakota, Izzy, and Toya followed Aisha into the clearing. After a few moments, the group caught up to the runners. They had caught six rabbits and were gathering them up and placing them in a pile at Alpha's feet.

"You all are just in time; the runners need to rest. You can help us carry these rabbits back to our den.

Together, we will celebrate our hunt and feast," Alpha said.

Izzy, Toya, Aisha, and Dakota each picked up a rabbit, and followed Alpha and the rest of the pack back to their den. Izzy stared in shock and surprise as Aisha tore into the rabbit meat with the rest of the pack. It seemed like her aversion to eating raw meat completely disappeared. Her sharp teeth ripped apart the meat with ease. Izzy and her friends ate until their bellies were bursting. They joined in on the storytelling and retelling of the day's events. It seemed like everyone had a story to tell from many different viewpoints. It reminded Izzy of the stories her father and his friends would tell after returning from a fishing trip.

"Aisha, Izzy, Toya, and Kay have shown us that they are brave wolves and therefore you are one of us.

You will join us in our ritual of life, because for us to live we must kill. So we must honor the rabbits."

Alpha and the other wolves began to gather the skulls and bones of the rabbits into a pile. Izzy and her friend followed the direction of the other wolves and began to pick up the bones and place them on the growing heap. The wolves then gathered in a circle around the bones. Alpha took an unusual spot and stood shoulder to shoulder with the other wolves.

"We will bow our heads to the rabbits because they have ascended far above us," he said as he and the other wolves bowed their heads. Izzy and her friends followed suit. After a few moments, out of the corner of her eye Izzy saw Dakota walk to the middle of the circle and let out a howl.

The rest of the pack followed her lead and began to howl. Alpha was the last to join. After a few minutes of howling, Alpha spoke.

"The circle of life is the great equalizer. Izzy, Toya, Kay, and Aisha, please step forward."

The wolf pack began to form two lines. Izzy and her friends joined Alpha at the front of the line.

"If you would like to join our pack you must be accepted by us all, from the greatest of us to the least among us. Once you have passed by us all and have been greeted first as friends and then as family, you will then take your place at the end of the line forever as family."

Izzy looked at Alpha and the rest of the wolf pack. She smiled at Dakota, who was standing at the back of the line. She remembered the last few days she spent with Dakota and tears began to well in her eyes.

"Alpha, we would like to join your pack, but we must go home. Mora is waiting for us and will turn us back into humans tonight. We will no longer be wolves," she cried.

"I know, but you don't have to be in wolf form to be wolf. You can change what is on the outside, but you can't change who you really are deep inside. You will be forever a part of our family no matter what form you take. You will forever be wolf," Alpha said.

At that moment, Izzy knew he was right. She walked down the line of wolves, starting first with Alpha. Each wolf greeted her by rubbing their head against hers. Finally, she got to the end of the line.

"Sister," Dakota whispered as she rubbed her head against Izzy's.

Once Izzy, Kay, Aisha, and Toya had taken their place at the end of the line, all the other wolves began to bark and howl.

Izzy stared up at the bright, white clouds as the sun warmed her fur. She could hear the steady breathing of her pack mates as they lounged in the sun all around her.

"It will be getting dark soon; you all must get back to Mora," Dakota said from somewhere next to her.

"You are part of our pack now, a few of us will join you and make sure you reach your destination safely," Alpha said.

"Okay, let's get going," Izzy said as she scanned the lounging bodies for Toya, Kay, and Aisha, who were so camouflaged with the other wolves it was hard for Izzy to spot them. Kay was the first one to pop her head up, followed by Toya and Aisha. Together with Dakota, Luna, and Alpha, the group headed up the mountain to Mora's cave.

Chapter 15
"Don't worry about me"

Mora was already outside of her cave, waiting for them.

"You're late! Look, the sun has already begun to set, you can already see the full moon," Mora said.

"Sorry, Mora, we got held up a little, but we are ready to go now," Izzy said.

"The time of day when a full moon and sun share the sky is very peculiar. It can be lucky and unlucky at the same time.

With luck on our side and the wind at our backs, we should be able to cover a lot of ground. We have a long way to go," Mora said. Izzy looked up at the faint transparent outline of the moon in the clear blue sky and the sun that was playing peek-a-boo behind the mountains. It made her think of the times when she played the game with her little brother.

I'm coming home, Drew.

"Keep your eye on the sky, I move swiftly," Mora said as she transformed into an owl once more and took off in flight. The group of wolves took off running down the mountain, trying their best to keep Mora in their sights.

Izzy loved the feeling of the wind ripping through her fur as she raced through the woods with her friends. She could see Alpha and Kay racing ahead of them. She marveled at how fast Kay was. Aisha was running shoulder-to-shoulder next to her, determined not to fall behind and to catch up with Kay. Dakota was keeping up with her on the right. Izzy could hear Toya and Luna following close behind them. The trees whizzed by as they tried their best to avoid the low-hanging branches. Kay showed off her parkour skills as she easily jumped and flipped over every fallen log with exaggerated and wholly unnecessary flair. Suddenly, Alpha and Kay stopped running. They sat in a clearing along a well-worn path. Izzy slowed so she didn't run into them. Mora swooped down from the sky and transformed back into her human form before her feet hit the ground.

"We are here. The human camp is just a little way down this path."

Izzy looked over the hill and could see the tops of a few RVs.

"You must hurry. Izzy, Kay, Aisha, and Toya, please gather around this stone."

Mora pointed to a small boulder next to the trail. Mora took the moonstone necklace off Izzy's neck and laid it on the stone. Izzy looked behind her to see that Aisha had not joined them.

"Come on, Aisha. We don't have much time," Izzy said.

Aisha walked over and stood behind Alpha.

"I'm not going."

Chapter 16

"What do you mean you're not going?" Izzy, Toya, and Kay asked in disbelief as they gathered around Aisha.

"There is nothing for me to go back to. You all have families that miss you and are looking for you. For the first time in my life, I actually feel like I'm part of a family. Don't worry about me, I'll be fine."

"How can you say that? You're my sister and you are a part of my family," Toya said.

“You are just saying that because you’re stuck dealing with me because your mom wanted to be a foster parent.”

“Yes, it was my mom's decision to become a foster parent, but from the moment you came into my life I have loved you like a sister.”

“Let’s be honest, I’m way better at being a wolf than a human.”

“You were there for me when the kids bullied me at school, we have fun playing together, I love helping you with your homework, you are the one I tell all my secrets to. I always felt so alone and depressed until you told me I was beautiful and should love myself more. I’m so grateful that my mom chose to become a foster parent because if she hadn't, I would never have met you. I know my family cares about you and loves you. Because I care about you. I know we all do." Toya wiped away a tear that rolled down her chin.

"She is right, we all care about you. You are our friend and a part of our family now. Just like the wolf pack, we are now bonded forever, and we won't leave someone we love behind," Izzy said.

"You are our sister, we love you. Please come home with us," Kay said.

Aisha stood before her friends with tears in her eyes. She never heard anyone tell her they loved her before, and now she had heard it three times.

"I'm so sorry for the way I have treated you all, especially you, Toya. All you have ever done was try to be nice to me and I just kept shutting you out. I was just scared.

I was scared of being tossed away again. I'm so sorry." Aisha sobbed.

"You don't have to fear that ever again," Toya said as they snuggled close to Aisha, wiping away her tears.

"The moon is highest now; if we are going to do this it must be now," Mora said.

Izzy, Kay, Aisha, and Toya quickly ran back to the stone. Izzy turned back just before reaching the stone.

"Dakota, I want to thank you so much for all your help. I'm truly going to miss you," Izzy said.

"You saved my life; I should be the one thanking you. You are a special girl. I won't say goodbye because I know we'll meet again someday, so I'll just say, see you later." Dakota rubbed her head against Izzy. She walked back to Mora and her friends, stopping one last time to look back at Dakota, Luna, and Alpha.

***

Izzy stared at her moonstone necklace as it began to glow in the moonlight. She could faintly hear Mora chanting a spell, but a fog crept over her senses. She could barely see Aisha, who was seated across from her. She began to feel very dizzy and light-headed as she struggled to keep her eyes open. Suddenly, Izzy heard the loud crack of gunfire. The sound immediately broke the fog of the spell and Izzy saw Mora quickly transform back into an owl and disappear into the treetops. Izzy whipped her head around as she heard three more gunshots. She watched as Alpha, Dakota, and Luna took off running into the woods.

"Are you okay?" she heard ranger Jeff ask as he shone a flashlight into her eyes. Izzy held her hands up to shield her eyes as she looked up to see two other rangers staring down at her. Immediately, Ranger Jeff took off his jacket and handed it to her. It was at that moment she realized she was completely naked. Izzy quickly covered herself with the jacket and looked to see that Kay, Toya, and Aisha were huddled together, sharing the jacket given to them by the other rangers. Izzy crept over to her friends as the rangers called for help on their radios.

"I didn't realize we were going to be naked! How are we going to explain this?" Izzy said.

"Don't worry, let me do the talking," Toya said as Ranger Jeff approached them.

"Are you all okay? We have the medics coming," he said.

"Yes, we are okay," Toya said.

"What happened to you out there? What happened to your clothes? How on earth did you survive the night?" Ranger Jeff hammered them with questions.

"We got lost and couldn't find our way back to the camp. We survived by eating berries. While we were walking in the woods we fell into the lake and got wet. We decided to take off our clothes so we could use our body heat to keep warm. Unfortunately, during the night, the rainstorm blew away all of our clothes that we left out to dry," Toya said as Kay, Izzy, and Aisha nodded in agreement.

"Well, you're very lucky. You could have gotten hypothermia. You could have died."

Izzy could see the flashing lights of the ambulances as they made their way up the trail.

Ranger Jeff left to direct the ambulances up the rocky trail.

"Wow, that was a really good story you spun," Kay said.

"I've been thinking about it for a while. I figured there would be a lot of questions."

Izzy and her friends were given blankets by the medics. They said goodbye and gave each other one final hug as the medics laid them on a gurney and loaded them each into the four ambulances.

"Where are my parents?" Izzy asked a ranger as she was pushed past him.

"Your parents are staying at a nearby hotel, they are being notified as we speak. You should see them soon," he said as he shut the ambulance doors.

Chapter 17
"What do you expect us to do?"

"Isadora, Isadora?"

Izzy heard a soft voice calling her name, and felt a gentle hand patted her shoulder. She opened her eyes slowly and looked into the face of a woman she had never met before. Izzy looked around and noticed a long curtain going across the room. Suddenly, the events from the night before flooded into her mind. She looked back at the woman. This time noticing her name tag and the stethoscope around her neck.

I'm in the hospital.

"I'm Nurse Mary. How are you feeling?"

"I'm fine, my arm is a little itchy." Izzy pointed to the needle in her arm.

"Sorry about that. When you came in you were a little dehydrated, so we put you on a saline drip. After you're finished with this bag, we can talk to the doctor about taking the IV out. How does that sound?"

"Okay. Have you heard from my parents yet?"

"Yes, they were here all night. I think they may have just stepped out for a moment to get some breakfast. Your little brother is adorable," Nurse Mary said as she wrote something down on Izzy's chart. "If you need anything, just push this button, otherwise I'll come back in a few hours to check on your IV. Try to get some sleep.

Here's the remote if you get bored."

"Thank you."

Izzy watched Nurse Mary pull the curtain back and walk out of the room. The door slammed behind her with a loud click. The room was completely silent except for the steady, soft beeping of the medical machine in the corner. Izzy was deciding whether she wanted to go back to sleep or watch TV, when she heard rustling in the corner of the room behind the window curtains. She peered closely at the curtains and saw a bunch of brown feathers sticking out of the bottom.

"Mora?" she said into the silence. The curtains began to move more and the figure behind the curtain grew larger until finally the curtain grew still again, and a delicate hand snaked its way through the thick folds of the fabric and pulled it apart to reveal Mora.

She stood in front of the window with the morning sun shining through her wavy, sandy-brown hair. She looked completely human this time and was wearing a dress she made to look just like the Kente fabric Izzy left in her cave.

"I thought they would never leave!" Mora said as she glided across the room with tiny steps.

"I was hiding there all night. I must have fallen asleep."

Mora sat on the edge of the bed.

"Why did you stay here? I thought I would never see you again," Izzy said.

"I have something important to tell you. Plus, you forgot this."

Mora pulled Izzy's moonstone necklace from her pocket and handed it to her.

"Thank you so much! I thought I lost it." Izzy placed the necklace around her neck.

"It's fully charged now. You should be able to talk with wolves again as long as you are wearing it."

Izzy twirled the stone around in her fingers. "What was so important that you needed to tell me?"

Mora took Izzy's hands into hers. "There was a problem with the spell, it was never completed."

"What! What do you mean it was never completed?" Izzy's eyes grew wide.

"The humans came shooting their guns, and they interrupted the spell. I never got to finish."

"So what does this mean for us? I feel fine."

Mora stood and walked over to the window.

"That's just it, I don't know what this means. 'vel never had a spell interrupted before." She sighed deeply.

Izzy looked at her hands, then lifted the blanket to look at her toes.

"I look normal, maybe it's nothing."

"Maybe it's nothing, or maybe on the next full moon you change back into a wolf... or maybe it's nothing," Mora said, looking over her shoulder with a head rotation that reminded Izzy she was not talking to a human.

"What? Can't you do another spell to fix it just in case?" Izzy said as she abruptly sat up in her bed.

"That would not be wise, it could make matters worse. I need to know what the effects of the spell are before I can do a new spell to fix it."

"So what do you expect us to do?"

"Don't worry. On the next full moon, we'll know what the side effects are and I'll fix it. You only have to wait a month." Mora tapped her long, sharp nails on the glass.

"A month! We'll be leaving soon. There's no way I'll be anywhere near here in a month." Izzy flopped back onto her pillow.

"Then I suggest you be careful during the full moon until you can get back here. You could be a danger to your family," Mora said as she tried to open the window.

"This can't be happening!"

"I assure you, it is."

Izzy rolled onto her side and watched Mora struggle with the window for a moment.

"Those windows don't open. You're going to have to walk out of here the same way you came in."

"Hmm, I got a lot of stares when I came in, I think it was this dress. Are you sure all humans wear dresses like this?"

"Well, it's definitely a fashion statement. Maybe lose the sleeves, next time if you don't want to turn heads."

"Thank you, and remember, be careful during the full moon, and get back here as soon as you can," Mora said as she walked out the door.

Izzy groaned. *How am I ever going to convince my parents to come camping ever again?*

Just then the door opened and her dad walked in, followed by her mother holding her brother Drew. They rushed to her bed.

"Izzy, you're awake!" Izzy's dad said.

"I was so worried about you! You scared me half to death! How are you feeling?" her mom asked.

"Are you hurt anywhere?"

"Calm down, please, I'm fine," Izzy said, hugging her parents. "I'm so sorry I worried you both like this. It must have been so awful for you all." Tears began to form in her eyes.

"Hush now, don't cry. You're okay, that's all that matters now," her mom said as she stroked Izzy's hair.

Izzy's brother crawled across the bed and reached out his tiny hand to wipe away her tears.

"Izzy," Drew babbled.

"Ah! He said my name!" she gasped as she scooped Drew up into her arms and buried her face into his neck. Izzy took a deep breath as she sighed; he smelled like milk and powder.

"I missed you so much," she whispered.

"Izzy, the nurse said you need to get as much rest as possible. If everything goes well today, we can go home tomorrow," Izzy's mom said as she fixed the blankets on her bed.

"Here is the lunch menu, circle everything you want, and I will give it to the nurse. Get some sleep, we will be back after lunchtime," Izzy's dad said, passing her a sheet of paper.

She looked at the lunch menu and tried to pick something that looked appealing. She thought about Dakota and the fish she taught her to catch and the berries they found. Nothing on the menu seemed to compare to that first meal as a wolf. Izzy took a deep sigh and circled the first thing on the menu, chicken salad on a rye roll.

"Here you go." Izzy handed the menu to her dad. He kissed her on the forehead. "Oh, I have a gift for you," he said as he handed her a magnet.

"What is this?" Izzy asked as she twirled the magnet around in her hands.

"It's a little souvenir from the haunted high school, remember that scary story we heard at the bonfire?"

"Yes!"

“While you were sleeping, we decided to stop by and check it out.”

“Wow, did you see any ghosts?”

“I don’t know, I felt an unusual breeze pass by me a few times.”

“That's so cool. Maybe we can go tomorrow.”

“Maybe, if we have time. Get some sleep now.”

Izzy watched as her family walked toward the door.

"Mom," Izzy said before her mom could shut the door. "Can you check on my friends, Aisha, Toya, and Kay?"

"I don't know if they will tell me anything since we’re not family, but I will see what I can find out. Don't worry, just get some sleep," Izzy's mom said as she flipped the light switch off and shut the door.

They are my family, Izzy thought as she closed her eyes.

Chapter 18
"Good news"

Izzy awoke to the sound of someone gently knocking on her room door.

"Come in."

Izzy's door opened and a man walked in pushing a cart.

"Lunchtime," he said as he handed Izzy a plate of food wrapped in clear plastic.

"Thank you," Izzy said as she watched him wheel the cart out of the room. Izzy finished up her food very quickly, she was much hungrier than she thought.

Just as she was finishing up, her family walked in.

"Hey, Izzy, how are you feeling?" her mom asked.

"I'm fine," Izzy replied.

"Glad to see you eating; I always hated hospital food," Izzy's dad said.

Izzy stretched out her arms and immediately her brother released himself from their mother and jumped into her arms. Izzy handed him a leftover potato chip from her lunch.

"Good news, the doctors said you can go home tomorrow," Izzy's mom said as she handed her a bag of clothes.

"That's great. Were you able to get any information about my friends?" Izzy asked as she looked at the new clothes her mom brought her.

"Not much, sorry. I did meet Kay's mom in the cafeteria. She is fine and will be heading home tomorrow also. I assume everyone is doing fine."

"I hope so. Aisha got really cold at one point. I was really afraid she would get hypothermia or something."

"You all were really lucky. I hope you learned a lesson to never stray from the group again," her dad said.

"I did, and I'm sorry for everything."

"Hey, we all make mistakes. The important thing is you all stayed together and survived. I'm proud of you for that," her dad said, hugging her.

"Oh, I almost forgot, Kay's mom gave me Kay's phone number," her mom said, handing her a small piece of paper. Izzy stared down at the crumpled paper.

"My phone! I lost my phone in the woods."

"Why did you take it anyway?" Izzy's mom asked.

"I was hoping to get a signal while on the hike. I still haven't heard back from Ana," Izzy said with a sigh.

"Don't worry about it. We'll get you a new phone when we get home. I'm sure she'll call you when we get back. You two could never go this long without speaking to each other."

"I don't... I don't even know if we are best friends anymore."

Just then Izzy heard another knock on the door.

"Come in," they all said in unison.

"Jinx!" Izzy yelled first.

It was Nurse Mary.

"How was your nap?" she asked.

"It was pretty good. I'm surprised I'm so tired."

"Well, I can only imagine what your body went through; being tired is to be expected after such an ordeal. Good news, I heard you will be going home tomorrow! So I can take this IV out for you, okay?"

"Thanks."

Izzy watched Nurse Mary remove the tape from her arm and gently pull the IV needle out. She then quickly taped a cotton ball over the tiny hole.

"There you go. There is a shower in your bathroom, feel free to use it if you want. The cafeteria staff will be around later to collect your tray; be sure to order your dinner. I recommend the meatloaf. Push the button if you need me."

"Thank you," Izzy replied as Nurse Mary left the room. Izzy visited with her family for the next few hours. They watched TV in between hearing stories about how Izzy and her friends survived by eating berries. Izzy wished she could tell her parents the truth about what happened, but she feared they would not believe her and think she was delusional. She didn't want to have to stay in this room any longer than she had to.

"Okay, we have to get back to the hotel. Visiting hours are over. We'll be back early tomorrow morning to check you out.

We have an early flight to catch," Izzy's mom said as she gently lifted a sleeping Drew off Izzy's bed. Izzy smiled as she watched her family leave. Her eyelids grew heavy.

I'll just take a quick nap before dinner, Izzy thought as she closed her eyes.

Chapter 19
"We just don't know what's going to happen"

Izzy was so eager to go home that by the time her parents arrived she had already showered, dressed, and eaten breakfast. Izzy and her parents arrived early at the airport. Izzy scanned the seats, looking for her friends.

"Who are you looking for?" Izzy's dad asked when he caught her frantically looking around the airport waiting area.

"Oh, I was just hoping to see my friends again, one last time."

"Well, it's likely they got on another flight," her mom said as they began to board the plane. Izzy sat down in the window seat and her father sat in the aisle seat next to her.

"I hope this middle seat stays empty," Izzy's dad said with a grin. Izzy smiled.

"I guess, meeting new people won't be so bad." Izzy looked out the window, she watched as the baggage handlers loaded everyone's luggage into the plane. Then she smelled it. Cotton candy bubble gum. At first, Izzy thought she imagined it as she continued to look out the window, but the sickeningly sweet smell wafted by her nose again.

"That is definitely cotton candy bubble gum," Izzy said as she looked up over the heads of the other passengers.

Then she saw it, a tuft of pink and black hair making its way down the aisle.

"Kay!" Izzy yelled as she stood up.

"Ouch!" Izzy winced and rubbed her head that she had managed to bang on the overhead compartment. Kay's eyes grew wide, and a big grin spread across her face, when she noticed Izzy waving at her.

"Izzy!" Kay said as she made her way down the aisle to Izzy's row.

"Dad, do you mind if Kay sits here?" Izzy asked as she pointed at the middle seat.

"No, not at all."

Izzy's dad stood as Kay scooted past him and sat next to Izzy.

"I was worried I wouldn't see you again."

"Me too. Have you seen Toya or Aisha?"

"Nope," Kay replied, snapping her gum.

"I have something important to tell you, but we can't talk now," Izzy whispered, gesturing to her dad who was leaning across the aisle playing with Drew. Kay nodded in understanding and settled back in her chair. "Gum?" Kay offered, holding out the pack of gum for Izzy.

"No, thanks."

Izzy waited until they were well into the flight and her dad put on his headphones to watch a movie before she spoke.

"Kay, Mora visited me while I was in the hospital," Izzy whispered.

"Really? Why?"

"She said the spell was interrupted but she doesn't know what that means for us."

"What?" Kay shouted.

"Shhh!" Izzy said, looking to see if her dad had been distured. But he had dozed off and was snoring softly.

"Yes, she said to be careful during the next full moon."

"So, what? She thinks we'll turn back into wolves during the next full moon?"

"She didn't exactly say that; we just don't know what's going to happen, maybe nothing." Kay ran her hands through her hair in frustration.

"What are we going to do?"

"I don't know, I'll figure something out. But we need to contact Aisha and Toya before the next full moon to warn them," Izzy whispered.

"They shouldn't be too hard to find if they have any social media accounts," Kay replied. "Okay. When we get home, your job will be to find a way to contact Toya and Aisha, and I'll figure out what to do about the next full moon," Izzy said.

"What are you two whispering about?" Izzy's dad said, making them jump.

"Nothing, we just didn't want to wake you," Izzy replied.

"Hmmm," Izzy's dad said, lying back in his chair and closing his eyes.

Izzy and Kay looked at each other and giggled.

"Let's watch a movie," Kay said.

"Sure, you pick," Izzy said.

Chapter 20
"It's the police"

Izzy dragged her bags into the house and collapsed onto the sofa. She was so exhausted from traveling.

"Hey, before you sit down, you might as well take your luggage upstairs," Izzy's mom yelled from the kitchen.

Izzy groaned and forced herself to stand. She grabbed her luggage and began to pull it up the stairs. She cringed after each thud of her suitcase hitting the stairs, but she was too tired to pick it up and carry it. When she finally made it to her room, she collapsed onto her bed.

"Hey, Izzy, how about pizza for dinner?" her mom yelled from downstairs.

"Sure!"

Izzy opened her suitcase and began to take her clothes out and place them in her hamper. Ding-dong. Izzy heard the doorbell.

Wow, that was fast.

Izzy heard the mumbles of her mother talking to someone at the door.

"Honey," her mom called her father to join her at the door. Izzy heard further mumbles at and grew curious.

That's not the pizza delivery.

Izzy walked to the top of the stairs to see if she could hear better.

“Izzy,” her mom called out to her just as she reached the top of the stairs.

“Yes?” Izzy said back.

“Come down here, please.”

Izzy slowly walked down the stairs, a feeling of dread washing over her with every step. She arrived at the bottom of the stairs. She could see her mother and father standing at the front door. Izzy’s mother turned to look at her and opened the door wider. Outside in the glow of the porch light, Izzy could see two police officers standing in the doorway.

“It’s the police, they want to speak with you,” Izzy’s mom said as she walked over to Izzy and placed her arms around her shoulders .

"It's Ana. She's missing."

The end

Order Book 2 of the Wolf Pack series!
The Missing Girl

Thanks for reading
If you have time to spare, a short review would be greatly appreciated.

Other books by Victoria Odoi-Atsem

Printed in Great Britain
by Amazon